Out of the Earth

Earlier and related novels by Colin Walker

INCOMPATIBILITY

THE GILDED CAGE

GO HOME REJOICING

Out of the Earth

Colin Walker

CONNOLLY & WILSON
Publishers

First published in the United Kingdom in 2002
by Connolly & Wilson

ISBN 0 9535655 1 3

Cover design: John I. Stanway

Printed and bound in Great Britain by
The Choir Press, Gloucester GL1 5SR

For Pippa

'He wearied me. He was too fond'.

George Eliot,
Middlemarch.

How happy could I be with either,
Were t'other dear charmer away.

John Gay,
The Beggar's Opera.

Chapter One

His arrival saved Kitty's life. Having gone behind the reception counter, she was on the point of writing a suicide note when she saw him coming up the half dozen steps that led from the promenade to the glass door with NEW LEAF HOTEL painted on it in gold capitals.

He wanted a room for the night.

'Is it just for yourself, Mr Dooley?' Kitty asked, watching him enter his name and address in the register. 'Or is your wife outside in the car?'

'The trouble and strife? She's under the floor boards. Haven't got one, sweetness. Is this all you want in the book or would you like a list of my previous convictions? No extra charge. I'm known to the police as Birmingham Bert, by the way.'

'Birmingham is where you live, but you've got a cockney accent. Is it just for one night, Mr Dooley?'

'Well, who in his right mind would want to stay longer in Redstone Bay? Be fair, my love!'

'October isn't the right time to see it. Wind and rain don't help and neither does the high tide banging away at the sea wall.'

'I didn't know the bleedin' place existed till half an hour ago, when I found there wasn't a sparrer's nest to be 'ad in Blackpool.'

'It's the lights. The illuminations. People come from all over.'

'One of the yokels mumbled something about a conference

somewhere. The Institute for Destitute Prostitutes, I shouldn't wonder. Any chance of a pint of bitter, sweetness? I'm fair dyin' o' thirst.'

'Go and sit in the lounge-bar, just behind you, while I take my outdoor things off. There's a log fire and the evening paper's just come.'

'I shall devour that immediately. I been wonderin' all day about the price of fat cattle and how the sale-of-work went on Sunday. Were you going out or coming in just now?'

Kitty smiled.

'Coming in,' she lied.

She hung her coat and silk headscarf on one of the pegs under the stairs and went up to the attic flat she shared with her husband and the Persian cat, sleek and imperial, who condescended to live with them. By the time she returned, she had brushed her black hair, dabbed a little powder on the snub nose that Frank liked to kiss and collected the cigarettes and matches she had left at her side of the bed in the belief that she would never need them again.

Charles Dooley was standing in the bay window, pipe in mouth, rocking on his heels and looking out over the rain-swept promenade and the heaving sea to the fog that hid the horizon. Born in London in 1923, he was now forty-five, making him twelve years older than Kitty. He was clean shaven, with brown hair and eyes and soft, pinkish, almost feminine skin. A little taller than average, he was portly from too much food, too many pints of bitter and too much time spent behind the wheel of his Citroën Light 15.

'What in the world brought you to this place?' he asked, as if unable to imagine a worse fate. 'Were you born here?'

'No. In Liverpool. Like my husband. I'm expecting him back from the library any time now. He bought the hotel from my Auntie Flo five years ago, when we married.'

'And turned over a new leaf. That name on your door's got to mean something.'

'Here's your beer and your room key. Will you want dinner this evening, Mr Dooley?'

Turning to face Kitty, Charles said he liked Chinese food and asked if there was 'a Chink place' in Redstone Bay. She replied that there was a Chinese restaurant opposite the Ninian Hotel, which he must have passed on his way in from Blackpool.

'We go there ourselves occasionally.'

'And you've survived.'

'You'll like it. Good food and lots of variety. Shall we sit for a moment? I could do with a smoke. That's nice tobacco you're smoking. Holland House, isn't it? The smell always reminds me of ice cream. I like to see a man with a pipe in his mouth. He looks solid and reassuring and happy to be at home with his wife and family.'

'You've thought that one through and no mistake. It must be those long dark evenings you have up here in the wild and woolly norf. What do I call you, by the way?'

'Mr and Mrs Hatfield. You're smiling and I don't blame you. I'd like everyone to call us Frank and Kitty, but Frank says first names are for friends. Kitty isn't in fact my real name, but it's the one I like. Only my mum and my husband call me Cath or Cathy - Catherine, if I've done something wrong. Someone very dear to me christened me Kitty.'

'One day you'll tell me about him. Will you have a drink with me?'

'I'd love a vodka and lime, but not this side of dinner. That's the rule we've made for ourselves, Frank and me. Dinner's at seven, if you change your mind, and it's just whatever we're having ourselves. Really speaking, this isn't a hotel. It's a guest house, or what used to be called a boarding house.'

The lounge-bar had seating for twenty or so on sofas and in armchairs recently given a new lease of life by the addition of chintz covers. Low tables for ashtrays and drinks were placed conveniently here and there. Carpets and curtains, like those in the dining room and conservatory, were of household quality and riotous colour combinations. Frank would have preferred the sober and sophisticated ambience achieved at the Ninian, but his Cathy liked what she had chosen and that mattered more to him than his own preferences.

She lit one of her Three Castles cigarettes and asked Dooley, with a smile and a squeak of amusement in her voice, what brought him to Redstone Bay on a cold and miserable end-of-season afternoon.

'You strike me as a traveller of some sort,' she added, 'but I don't think you're a rep.'

'I take that, sweetness, as a compliment.'

Dooley shared the widespread British distaste for sales representatives, maintaining that they rode round in cars all day and got their money for nothing. He asked Kitty if she had ever heard of Ketter's department stores and then said, without waiting for a reply, that he was their Clerk of Works.

'I guessed you were in charge of people – a police inspector perhaps or a fire prevention officer, like the one who comes here.'

'I cover England and Wales. Another bloke does Scotland.'

'What a lovely life! – being in a different town every day. Frank used to work for Ketter's in Liverpool. He was a salesman in the carpet department. Or was it furniture? What does a Clerk of Works do?'

'What does he do? As little as possible. He keeps a surveyor's eye on the buildings, inside as well as out, and engages and supervises contractors when repairs or alterations are called for. I was at the Liverpool store for three days last month and stayed at that hotel opposite.'

'Graham's.'

'Is that what it's called? What a boring place!'

'Most people think it's the best in Liverpool.'

'Lord protect me from the worst! The water was cold, the plates was cold . . . Oh, dearie me!'

Kitty was smiling, tickled by Dooley's pronunciation of water as woh-er and cold as coh. Laughing now, she asked if he had complained, certain that he had.

'To the manager. Always start at the top. I don't like hotels all that much. If I can get finished in a day, I drive back to Elsie. She's my landlady. Treats me like a toff she does.'

Watching Kitty over at the other side of the fire, Dooley smiled and lightened the conversation with a chuckle that shook his shoulders. He was getting to like what he saw: curly black hair, blue eyes sparkling with merriment and a neat little turned-up nose above an impish smile. At thirty-three, childless Kitty Hatfield, still with clear skin and teeth of Hollywood whiteness, retained the figure of her youth without ever dieting or performing physical exercises.

Dooley said: 'Tell me about this new leaf caper. It's got me interested. Don't ask me why.'

'This place was called One Eighty when Frank bought it from my Auntie Flo. That's its street number. The name-change came about because we were both making a fresh start. Frank was divorcing his first wife, Clare, and I'd just finished with someone else.'

'Someone else bein' the geezer who christened you Kitty, I shouldn't wonder.'

'Eleven out of ten. You look as if you'd like another pint, Mr Dooley.'

'I have that look permanently, Mrs Hatfield.'

The 'geezer's' name had been Clive Rolls, an erstwhile military policeman who had been shot dead in the hallway of his Liverpool dancing school by a man whom he had long ago beaten and crippled in a guardroom cell in Egypt. Only hours before his murder and following a long and turbulent courtship, Clive had asked Kitty to marry him. He had talked of buying One Eighty from her Aunt Flo and it had been his idea - not Kitty's, as Kitty had led Frank to believe - that the name be changed to the New Leaf Hotel. She rarely mentioned Clive to her husband, although the two men had been acquainted, but never a day passed without her thinking of him or looking at the photograph that she kept hidden from Frank.

Handing Dooley his pint before resuming her seat and lighting another cigarette, Kitty asked what time he would like breakfast next morning.

'Eight o'clock?' he ventured.

'Earlier if you like. Breakfast is from seven, when Frank gets back from his jogging. We often have reps staying and they like an early start. I do assure you, Mr Dooley, that they're not all one-to-two-and-an-hour-for-lunch types.'

'Try convincing me, sweetness.'

'We like having them. They're cheerful and easy talkers and we sometimes sit round the fire with them in this room after dinner. They have amusing tales to tell.'

'Eight o'clock'll do me in the morning. Jogging's something I should be doing too. When the doctor bloke took my blood pressure last week, he told me to lose a stone. I said I'd throw one into my neighbour's garden. He didn't like that. We do not joke with Doctor – even in 1968.'

Kitty laughed. She was finding Dooley attractive, despite his arrogance, his mouthful of ultra-white NHS teeth and his unhealthy physical bulk. He was breezy and relaxed, his informality reflected in his black leather jacket, his black shirt with mother-of-pearl buttons, his silver tie, black trousers and black slip-on shoes with a decorative silver chain across the instep.

'So where are you going tomorrow?' she asked, feeling an interest in his affairs. 'Home to Birmingham?'

'Back to Blackpool to meet Maurice Zerdin, my flooring contractor. Heard of them, have you? They've got a lorry so old it must once have had a geezer with a red flag walking in front of it. Maurice loves it. I think it stinks. I'm meeting him to sign off some work his blokes are doing for me at the Blackpool store – always supposing, of course, I approve it.'

'But of course, Mr Dooley. How often d'you get up this way?'

'Call me Charles.'

Kitty didn't.

'How often do I get to Blackpool, sweetness? As seldom as possible. My annual inspection isn't till January. I'm here now because changes to the counter layout mean the linoleum has to be stripped out and renewed.'

'And what brought you to the New Leaf Hotel might I ask?'

'What brought me to Kitty Hatfield? A stroke of good fortune. There's your answer, sweetness.'

Charles was smiling at Kitty round his pipe. She returned his smile and told him not to call her that when her husband was present.

Dooley spoke again.

'The store manager said to try Redstone Bay after ringing up half a dozen Blackpool hotels. Yours was the first along the promenade that didn't look as if it had a corpse laid out in the front room.'

'We stay open till the middle of December and reopen on the first Monday in February. We need that break after the summer season.'

'Needless to say, you don't take it locally with the Clutterbucks and the Ramsbottoms. You fly off to the ski slopes or the Costa Plenty, I shouldn't wonder.'

'Will you believe me when I say we've never been out of England? I've never even been to London. Frank's only passed through, when he was doing his National Service. He's an armchair traveller, my husband, who won't even learn to drive a car. When he isn't working – and he works very hard, I'll say that for him – he sits reading and eating fruit in the conservatory while I watch telly in here or in the attic flat. At first we lived in the basement, where we had a lovely view of dogs cocking their legs up against the area railings, but it was gloomy and depressing. Joyce lives there now with her little girl, Isobel. Joyce is our helper.'

Airy and compact, the attic flat caught the morning sun at the back and the westering sun at the front, and for a time it had checked the creeping despair that Kitty managed to hide even from Frank behind her playful disposition and frequent laughter. She had made it homely and inviting with her liberal use of colour, with flowers in every room and with goldfish and a rubber plant in what she called the lounge and her husband called the sitting room.

Kitty was heartened now when, the talk having turned to books and television, Dooley told her that he enjoyed watching sitcoms and never read anything except his pay slip. 'I agree with the bloke who called books a bloodless substitute for life,' he stated. 'They should all be buried at midnight in unconsecrated ground.'

Kitty replied: 'I could see Frank smiling slowly if you said that to him. He has a lovely smile.'

'But you're not in love with him, Kit. Were you ever?'

Kitty lowered her eyes.

'Was I ever what?'

'In love with Frank.'

'No. I'm here because the one I wanted was killed. I've never taken to Redstone Bay. The people hereabouts –

especially the faded blazer brigade, with their dusty suede shoes and hair that needs cutting – seem to think they're something special, when all they've got is a fake accent and an overdue account at the dairy. Redstone Bay is known in Liverpool as Debtors' Retreat.'

'You'd like to be back in Liverpool.'

'I'm sorry we ever left it. My mum still lives there. So does Frank's first wife and her husband, Nick, and the twins. We go to them for Christmas dinner and they come to us for New Year. Unfortunately, the Beeching axe fell on our railway station, which means a taxi to Preston to catch the Liverpool train and the same thing coming back.'

'Expensive.'

'Inconvenient too. Nick and Clare have a car, so it's easier for them. Here's my husband coming now.'

'I'll get my case out of the Cit.'

'I've given you the single room over the hall so's you'll have a view over the sea. If you want to call your girlfriend, the phone's on this floor under the stairs. I'm sure she's waiting to hear from you.'

'No girlfriend, sweetness. Just finished with one. Or shall I say she finished with me?'

'Come and meet Frank. Or shall I say Mr Hatfield? No. He's very nice.'

They found him lustily wiping his feet in the hall, some library books tucked under his left arm. His charming smile, never absent for long, widened his generous mouth and brightened his blue eyes as Kitty introduced him to Charles Dooley. She left them talking about Ketter's and went through to help Joyce prepare dinner for herself and Frank and the two representatives and one retired couple who were dining in.

2

'Frank, I've just remembered: I forgot to give Mr Dooley a front door key,' Kitty lied, the truth being that she had deliberately omitted to do so. 'You should put one on each of the bedroom keyrings, then guests could let themselves in.'

'And have a duplicate made and use it later to come in and

help themselves. Remember Bunny Littler?' Frank asked, smiling. 'That's what he used to do. Leave me to wait up for Chummy, Cath. You slide off to bed.'

'No. It's my mistake and besides I've got some mending to do. That little clergyman who stayed in number eight – the one whose breath smelt like a choked lavatory, you said – tore one of his sheets. Either that or they did it at the laundry and didn't let on.'

It was close to eleven o'clock and the couple were alone in the dining room, setting tables for next morning's breakfast. All twelve were permanently laid with gingham cloths, red-and-white alternating weekly with blue-and-white, and each had a clutch of condiments in the centre – Heinz Tomato Ketchup, Daddies Sauce and Sarson's Vinegar, together with salt and pepper in yellow-and-green plastic cruets and a jar of Colman's English Mustard.

Frank said, positioning the knives and forks: 'Talking of Bunny Littler, you and I are invited to tea the day after tomorrow at Osprey Court.'

'Friday . . .'

'In the afternoon.'

'I didn't think we knew anyone in Millionaire Mansions.'

'We do now, Cath. Lady called Gloria Raby – separated wife of Peter Raby and once my sister Dorothy's best pal. She was Gloria Brown in those days.'

'Where does Bunny Littler fit in?'

'He used to drive one of Raby's hire cars. Call it the association of ideas. Littler equals Raby, Raby equals Littler.'

'I never liked him. He was a bad influence on Clive Rolls. He's not here in Redstone Bay, is he?'

'I don't know where he is, love, and we won't mention him again. To get back to the point of the story, Gloria's been living in Osprey Court since her marriage to Raby fell apart. It's nigh on twenty years since we last came face to face, but we recognised each other at once this afternoon and she gave me a lift home from the library in her splendid car. A BMW. The biggest they make. She's been ill, she tells me, and she's living now with a woman who is half nurse half companion.'

Kitty had gone quiet, silenced by her thoughts. With her

thumb on the light switch, she looked round the room and agreed with Frank that they had left everything ready.

He followed her into the lounge-bar, which was empty of people, made up the log fire and placed the guard in front of it.

'Sure you want to stay up for Chummy, Cath?'

She had her back to him.

'You don't like him, do you?' she asked.

She was drawing the full-length curtains and the squeak of amusement had returned to her voice.

'He's a low-grade Londoner,' Frank replied. 'All piss and wind. Anything we know that he doesn't isn't worth knowing.'

Kitty laughed.

'He'll be away in the morning.'

Frank continued: 'The most ignorant London labourer considers himself innately superior to the most distinguished provincial. Did he say where he was going?'

'The pictures.'

'The Regent no doubt. To see Elvis Presley. Fit only for squealing girls. A man whose face contains everything except the light of intelligence.'

'I think he's rather nice. Pop off to bed, old boy, and give that brain of yours a chance to cool down. Chummy's probably treating himself to a Chinese supper opposite the Ninian.'

'What about this tea with Gloria Raby?'

Kitty was looking for something.

'Have you seen my cigarettes?' she asked.

'On the bar. You don't sound too enthusiastic. Why is that? You've often said you'd like to see inside Osprey Court.'

'Friday afternoon might be awkward, Frank, because Joyce has got a dentist's appointment and I've said I'll meet Isobel from school.'

'D'you mind if I go on my own?'

'Of course not. You can tell me what it's like.'

'The reason being that Gloria's going to lend me a newspaper cutting about my sister. She's dead.'

'Dorothy?'

'Fell downstairs at her home in London. Two years ago.'

'And you've only just heard?'
'This afternoon.'
'Why weren't you told at the time?'
'If I know Dorothy, she never told anyone she had a brother.'
'She wanted to be a writer, didn't she? She left Liverpool after your mother died.'
'Gloria says she had a big success. But not under her own name. She wrote schoolgirl stories under the name of Mary Orchard.'
'I've never understood families who don't keep in touch with one another. It's inhuman. I'd love to have a brother or sister to come and stay.'
'It was Dorothy who dropped me, Cath, not the other way round. She was always a loner, always a queer fish. She did the same to Gloria. The last time I saw my sister was at Lime Street Station in 1950, when she was headed for a new life in London and I was about to vanish into the RAF. I can't be expected to have any feelings for someone who had none herself.'
Kitty was shaking her head in bewilderment.
Frank said: 'Gloria's my last link with my family, because she sometimes called for Dorothy when we all lived in Liverpool and she remembers my mother and father. It'll be interesting to see what she's got to show me.'
'Mmm.'
'Right, Cath, I'm off. See you in the morning. Sure you're all right on your own?'
'He'll be here any minute.'
'Leave the outside lights on till you're coming up to bed.'
'All right.'
Kitty went through to the kitchen to fetch her mending while Frank busied himself with bolts and switches before calling 'Goodnight, love' and making his way upstairs.

3

Alone, Kitty settled herself in the warmth of the log fire, where her thoughts turned yet again to Clive Rolls, the lost love whom she had met when only sixteen at the Tower Ballroom in New Brighton and who had started calling her Kitty after convincing himself and almost convincing her that they would 'capture the attention of the world' as CLIVE ROLLS & KITTY, ballroom dancers. Their career was brief and unspectacular, peaking in 1954 with the award of a bronze medal and thereafter existing only in the alcoholic haze into which Clive frequently withdrew.

By a sad irony, the attic flat at the New Leaf Hotel so much reminded Kitty of Clive's flat above his Liverpool dancing school that it had the opposite of the desired effect, worsening instead of easing her carefully concealed depression. Clive had lived alone. Kitty had spent her free time assisting him as an unpaid teacher, sleeping with him at weekends but otherwise living with her widowed mother only two or three streets away.

Following his murder, there were reports in the Merseyside papers about repeated assaults on prisoners during his war service in Egypt; but these, she had decided, were exaggerated if not invented in the interests of selling copies. Everyone of her acquaintance who had known Clive Rolls had spoken well of him. He himself had longed to be a better person. Many were the times he had told Kitty of his desire to purify himself by stopping smoking, drinking and using coarse language. He had even fretfully admitted, after consuming the best part of a bottle of Lemon Hart rum, that he should have been a priest or even a knight of the Order of the White Heather, leaving the easily fooled Kitty with the belief that there really was such an order. As to the infidelity of which she had always suspected him, she was prepared to believe that this was encouraged and even engineered by Bunny Littler, who had resented Kitty's intrusion into his friendship with Clive.

For eight years she had tried with increasing desperation to get Clive to marry her, but always he had parried her attempts with reminders of the age difference ('I'm old enough to be your father, Kitten'), of his distaste for the sexual act ('as sickly as the coupling of dogs'), and of his dislike of children. He used to call them an expensive nuisance. But Kitty was unwavering in her belief that marriage and parenthood would have swept away all his objections.

It was during her afternoon rests, when cast down by memories and tormented by her longing for a family, that Kitty's thoughts turned ever and again to suicide. Triggered finally by the discovery of her first grey hair, the decision to end her life came less than one hour before Charles Dooley entered it. That afternoon, instead of smoking and staring at the ceiling, she lay on her stomach with her pretty face in the pillow, her small hands tightened into fists by the prospect of drowning, and composed in her mind the note that she would leave on the reception counter for her husband to pick up on his return from the lending library.

Sorry to leave you like this, Frank, when you've always been so good to me. Goodbye, my dear, and thank you for everything. If you wonder why I've done it, I have to admit what I think you've known all along. I've never forgotten Clive.

Neither had Kitty's mother, but for different reasons. Mrs Osborne had never liked Clive Rolls, dismissing him as effeminate and a selfish bachelor. No praise was too high, on the other hand, for Frank Hatfield, whom she regarded as an ideal husband, supportive and considerate. 'You've got a man in a million there,' she regularly informed her daughter. 'I could see your father helping me the way Frank helps you, and I don't think! If you'd married your precious Clive Rolls, he'd have had you waiting on him hand and foot, mark my words.'

Calm, pleasant, dependable, predictable – Frank was these and more, but Kitty had from the first found him uninteresting and even slightly ridiculous. He had pleaded with her to go out with him before his marriage to Clare Mason and she had done so with Clive's permission and in the vain hope of making the older man more disposed to marry her. Frank's marriage, forced on him by Clare's unintended pregnancy, had ended his pursuit of Kitty but not his love for her. Five years later, the death of his infant son and consequent weakening of the bond between himself and Clare had coincided with

Clive's murder and the end of Kitty's chance of becoming Mrs Rolls. Clare and Frank had parted - Clare to marry Nick Pound and bear his children, Frank to make his bid for Kitty Osborne.

Kitty had consented to marry him because by then she was twenty-four and deeply anxious to become a wife and mother. That conception eluded her didn't bother Frank, except in so far as it made her restless with frustration. He was happy with or without children. He had his Cathy and was content with a life that was quiet and uneventful, a life without change or achievement, a life lived largely in the imagination. When mentally preparing for suicide, Kitty told herself that Frank would mourn her passing, but at thirty-eight he was young enough to meet someone else and, on the practical side, he could easily afford to employ additional help in running the hotel. He would still have his jogging, his swimming, the reading that increasingly occupied his leisure hours, and the adult keep-fit class that he conducted every Friday evening at the Parish Hall in Redstone Village. He was a man of diverse and expanding interests, most of them passive and all of them solitary. Kitty's, on the other hand, had narrowed over the years to only one; and until the advent of Charles Dooley, she had seen no hope of its being satisfied.

Chapter Two

With her husband asleep in his half of the bed and all save Dooley gone to their rooms, Kitty finished her sewing, refreshed her make-up from the spare powder compact she kept in the kitchen and settled again beside the lounge fire. She switched on the television, lit a cigarette and began reading the feature story in her weekly magazine, *Sweethearts*, which she called her book despite Frank's kindly rebuke at her misuse of the noun. Kitty read and smoked in characteristic posture – sitting forward from the waist, the magazine open in her lap, her left elbow on her left knee, her left hand slotted into her hair.

He arrived at midnight.

Hearing him mounting the steps, Kitty threw away her magazine and hurried to unlock the glass door for fear he would ring the bell and bring her husband downstairs.

'Sorry, sweetness! I wasn't watching the time.'

His brown eyes were asking Kitty if she was angry with him, and his smile was sheepish – the smile of a boy who's been caught in the pantry by an indulgent parent.

'My fault,' Kitty assured him. 'D'you want anything from the bar before I leave you?'

'Must you, Kit?'

'Shhh! Redstone Bay is asleep.'

'I like being with you.'

'Here's your room key. Is there anything you want?'

'I'd cheerfully maul a pint of Reklaw's bitter. But only if you'll have a vodka and lime with me.'

'Well, okay. Go through to the fire while I lock up and switch the outside lights off. Did you like the picture?'

No answer.

Kitty followed Dooley into the lounge, where the light from two standard lamps, one at each side of the chimney breast, seemed uncommonly bright after the dimness of the hall, lit only by a pilot light.

He was facing her and smiling his approval.

'Is this the Kitty I was talking to this afternoon or an identical twin? The clothes . . .'

'I've only changed into a skirt and blouse and an old pair of court shoes.'

'Yes, but what a difference! I love women who look like women.'

'Slacks and a turban and flatties are more practical in the daytime. Both of us like to have a change in the evening. Sit down and tell me about the picture.'

'I didn't go. Went to Liverpool instead.'

'Liverpool!'

'It's only an hour in the Cit. I went into the pub next to the cinema and had a game of darts with one of the hayseeds. He said there was greyhound racing at Stanley Stadium.'

'So you just drank up and went!'

Kitty's eyes were shining with amused admiration. To one accustomed only to the occasional railway journey, a car trip to Liverpool (and an impromptu one at that) seemed daringly adventurous. And here was this man, this Charles Dooley, who could alter his plans in response to a casual remark and see nothing unusual in doing so! Kitty was used to Frank, who planned everything in advance, who never ran out of supplies and who had a time and place for everything.

She carried the drinks from the bar to the log fire, where she and Dooley took their seats at either side of the hearth.

'Did you win?' she squeaked, still admiring him with merry eyes.

'I think I broke about even, Kit. Cigarette?'

'Oh, thanks. Thought you were a pipe man.'

'Both. Sometimes a cigar. You need to relax to enjoy a pipe. Cigarettes are handy when I'm driving. Where's Brother Frank?'

'Gone to bye-byes.'
'Decent bloke, that.'
'Solid gold.'
'But not the last word.'
'I want children. I've always wanted them. It's not Frank's fault. He fathered a boy with Clare. So it can only be me.'
'Maybe you'd click with a different man.'
'We've tried everything else. Two doctors. An old herbalist who once stayed here. Even a psychiatrist. No luck. Tell me about yourself.'
'Charles.'
'You live a sailor's life, so you must've had lots of girls.'
'I've had my share, Kitty.'
'Tell me about the one you've just finished with. Or did you say she finished with you? I forget.'
'Mary Singleton. Different from any other girl I've ever met in the whole of my life. Too different, as I discovered when I met her parents.'
'You were in love with her. So it was Mary who ditched you, wasn't it?'
'I don't know if I was in love or not.'
'Oh, come on! We all know the test. You're in love with someone if you want to be with them all the time. Simple.'
'Mary and me were complete opposites. Mary was like what schoolmistresses was when I was a nipper. Bobbed hair. No make-up. No interest in clothes. She brightened up a bit after we'd been going out together for a while and even bought her first pair of high heels.'
Kitty hugged her knees and smiled.
'She wanted to please you. What did she look like? Have you got a photo of her?'
'I threw them on the fire one night.'
'And now you wish you hadn't. You *were* in love, weren't you?'
'As my boss would say, polishing his glasses with his tie, "That's a statement, Charles, not a question." What did Mary look like? Average height, nicely put together, smooth clear skin, lovely tapering hands. Eyes that sometimes looked grey

and sometimes green. Very well-spoken. Not like Yours Truly. No accent and never used slang.'

'Sounds prim.'

'Certainly proper. I once called trousers strides and she didn't know what I meant.'

'In Liverpool we call them kecks.'

'When I explained, she frowned and said "It must be a dialect word, dear." And then she pressed my hand as if to say I wasn't going to be caned.'

'Unless it happened again,' Kitty said, laughing. 'Where did you meet this frump? Not in a pub, that's for sure, and not at the greyhound races.'

'She worked for a firm of architects in Birmingham. Still does, I shouldn't wonder. Secretary to Kelvin Rill, the senior partner. We used to see each other at site meetings when Ketter's were having a new store built in Coventry. Mary took the minutes. She was twenty-five. I gave her a lift one day back to their offices on Hadley Road when Kelvin was having to go to the airport to collect his wife and I asked her if she'd come out with me that same evening.'

'But Mary-Mary was quite contrary. She said she was washing her hair, but in such a way as not to discourage you from trying again.'

'No. She didn't play hard to get. That came later. But it's what I was expecting her to say. Either that or "I'm seeing my friend tonight".'

'So where did you take her? To evensong?'

'I suggested a drive and a drink somewhere, but she said she'd rather go for a walk because it was a nice evening, and we ended up standing in front of the house where some actress or other had lived.'

'I'll bet it wasn't Marilyn Monroe.'

'Can't remember the name. I got Mary into a little pub eventually and she told me all about this actress bird while she sipped her ginger beer and Yours Truly started on the pints. You'd have thought they'd been friends, the way she was carrying on.'

'Mary's sounding less and less like your type. She might've suited Brother Frank, as you call him,' Kitty mused, with a glance at the door she had left half open. 'He's always learning something.'

'She knew a lot about things that don't matter. Know what I mean?'

'Like Frank.'

'Mary could go on about concerts and picture galleries and that sort of stuff. I've remembered the name of the actress bird. Faith Winkler.'

'I can't see her in *Coronation Street* with a name like that.'

'On the stage. Before your time. Probably before mine.'

'Tell me about Mary's mother and father. I'll switch the television off. What were they like? Middle class, that's for sure – maybe even upper. But the genuine article. Not the would-bes we have in Redstone Bay.'

'Very stiff. We'd been going out together for months before I got through the gates, let alone as far as the front door.'

Mary Singleton neither smoked nor drank nor frequented dance halls. Like her parents and the brother who lived in London, she belonged to the Anglican church, did voluntary work for it and helped raise money through coffee mornings and whist drives. She liked Charles to take her for walks and to the cinema, where they held hands, to a coffee bar afterwards and, eventually, to kiss her in the Cit at the end of the evening. On the solitary occasion when she had lingered and Charles, emboldened, had attempted to fondle her, she had been not angry but profoundly shocked. He had driven home convinced that his rashness had cost him Mary's friendship; but she had agreed to its resumption after a break to mark her disapproval and she referred to his advance only once more, weeks later, when she said that such intimacy was permissable only within marriage.

'What a pain in the neck!' Kitty exclaimed, laughing. She was already beginning to resent Mary and to see her as a rival for Dooley's attention. 'D'you still see her or is it over for keeps?'

'Kaputt. I haven't clapped eyes on Mary since we parted.'

That wasn't true. More than once, from behind the wheel of his parked car, Charles had watched her leaving work at the end of the day and wondered if he should approach her.

'You're sorry, aren't you?'

'I thought all girls were the same, Kit, till I met Mary. You chatted them up at a dance, perhaps took them for a drink, and ended up snogging in a lay-by.'

'You'd never have been happy with such a prude. You were worlds apart. Mary was living in the Ice Age.'

'Maybe that was the attraction. I promised to cut out boozing straight from work and gambling too, except on the classics, but that was all. No one was going to tell me what to do and when to do it.'

'Mary didn't like that,' Kitty concluded, with satisfaction in her smile and voice. 'Or were you supposed to call her Miss Singleton?'

'Oddly enough she did like it. I thought I'd lost her all over again when I said it, but she pressed my hand and said she'd lose respect for me if I turned into her puppet. "I like a man to be a man" was what she said. We talked of getting engaged.'

Then he met her parents.

For the first and only time, he drove his car through the black wrought iron gates topped with gold spear-heads and left it beneath the drawing room windows. It was Sunday and he was invited to luncheon. Hitherto, he had parked in the road, where Mary would join him at the appointed hour.

'It was comical in a way, because when she came out of her front door on the dot of half past seven, I couldn't help thinking of the cuckoo popping out of one o' them clocks just when it strikes. Know what I mean? I can see Mary now, walking towards the old Cit down the gravel drive, smiling at me and nodding and with her head on one side.'

The Singletons, complete with cook, maid and chauffeur-gardener, lived in the Egremont district of Birmingham, only a few minutes' walk from Hadley Road, where houses were described as gentlemen's residences and fetched between one and two million pounds. Theirs was long and low, made of rustic brick, with leaded windows in granite surrounds. The close-cropped lawns were sharply defined and brightened by circular flower beds. There were several copper beeches, a double garage containing a pearl-over-black Daimler Regency, and an assortment of out-buildings covered with ivy.

A maid in black and white opened the door, and there was Mary advancing along the hall, smiling her warm approval and saying 'You're an angel for coming.' But a different Mary. Gone were the formless tweeds and sensible shoes. Fresh from church like Doctor and Mrs Singleton, she was exquisite in powder blue silk and high heels, with platinum and sapphires at wrist and throat.

'Come along, dear. Father's in the drawing room.'

A retired anaesthetist and still a lay magistrate, the doctor was known behind his back as Wuthering Heights. He was tall and gaunt, rigid and coldly observant, with enough of the Potsdam cavalry officer about him to make Charles exclaim to himself 'All this geezer needs is a monocle and a bleedin' sabre scar.'

The doctor rose, Saturday's *Financial Times* dangling from his left hand.

'Mr Dooley,' he said, quietly, and with no move to shake hands. Face and voice alike were totally devoid of expression. 'Won't you sit down?'

'Don't mind if I do,' admitted Charles, loud and jovial, adding: 'Pleased to meet you.'

He bumped down with a sigh into a leather armchair while the older man regained his and Mary chose the sofa that faced the coal fire.

'Mother will be down in a moment, then sherry will be served,' she said, reassuringly.

'Nice one. Nice one,' Charles responded.

The doctor returned to his reading as Dooley, using heartiness to mask increasing unease, treated Mary to a lengthy description of how he had been followed by a police car, stopped and booked for speeding.

'Oh, how awful for you! Where was this, dear?' Mary asked, indulgently. 'Was it just now?'

She regretted Dooley's new outfit, knowing that the combination of navy serge, brown suede shoes, white nylon shirt and glossy red tie would not endear him to her parents. Her father, in sober contrast, wore a faultlessly tailored suit of clerical grey worsted, a white-and-grey striped shirt, black leather shoes and a maroon silk bow tie with matching socks and floppy display handkerchief.

'I thought Mr Dooley looked like a convalescent private soldier in his red, white and blue,' Mrs Singleton was to chortle later in her old, wobbly voice. 'That's how I remember them looking after the Great War.'

She entered the drawing room only moments ahead of the promised sherry, reacted warmly to Charles's repetition of 'Pleased to meet you' and immediately began talking with fluency and animation of music and literature.

Did Mr Dooley play an instrument?

'I've been known to play the fool.'

Who was his favourite composer?

Charles hesitated.

'Oh, come on!' Mrs Singleton urged. 'We all have at least one, Mr Dooley. Stravinsky? Shostakovich perhaps?'

'I like Mantovani.'

'I like him too,' Mary said, approvingly.

Her mother moved on quickly into literature, asking Dooley to remind her to show him the library after luncheon. Meanwhile, had he read Mulsanne's latest novel? No? An English translation was soon to appear, but she and Doctor, unable to wait, had already enjoyed it in the original French.

'Nice one. Nice one,' declared Charles.

'Let us into the secret of your own preferences, Mr Dooley,' Mrs Singleton persisted, with increased enthusiasm. 'Being on the Bench, Doctor sometimes relaxes with a detective story, don't you, dear? He favours Anthony Quinnis's novels about the Two Smart Men. But now you'll surprise us all by saying that Proust tops your list or Cynthia Justin Bourn.'

'Mother is a writer herself, Charles,' Mary said, adroitly coming to his rescue. 'She's written monographs of Helen Waddell and Siegfried Sassoon and they've been rather well received. I don't expect Charles gets much time for reading, Mother. Tell Mother and Father about your work, Charles. It's always interesting to hear about other people's occupations.'

Mrs Singleton responded with fervour, saying 'Ah, yes! Our daughter tells us you're a clerk, Mr Dooley.'

'Charles is a Clerk of Works, Mother,' Mary corrected, gently. 'It's not quite the same thing.'

Dooley was still noisily describing his duties as the party moved into the dining room. He stopped abruptly at a discreet signal from Mary. Then, after Doctor Singleton had said grace, he fell to recounting his experiences as oxtail soup gave way to roast beef with Yorkshire pudding, boiled potatoes, carrots and broccoli. He never forgot the occasion. He took away a memory of polished rosewood and Britannia silver, heavy carpets, curtains with swags and tails, a disconcerting array of crystal and cutlery, a maid moving soundlessly between sideboard and table, and the drowsy Westminster chimes of a clock in another room marking quarters that seemed like hours. And dominating all was the doctor's arctic stare – the stare that seldom spared him and was capable even in recollection of turning his stomach – and the busily attentive Mrs Singleton, chubby and bejewelled in green velvet and ginger wig, greeting Charles's revelations with squeals of delight and astonishment. Husband and wife between them were giving him his first experience of bruising condescension, and only by reminding himself that they were northerners did he manage to preserve a remnant of self-esteem.

Mary caught his eye, smiled and slightly shook her head when, addressing him as guv'nor, he asked her father what penalty he could expect for his speeding offence.

A pause.

'I suggest you wait and see,' came the doctor's cold reply.

'Mary has a brother, Roderick, you know, and we were all hoping he would be with us this weekend,' Mrs Singleton revealed, her verve undiminished. 'He would have loved your stories, Mr Dooley. He's at the Foreign Office, you know, and he was called abroad at short notice.'

'Trouble with the fuzzy-wuzzies in Bonga Bonga Land?' Charles demanded, lustily. He banged the table with his fist and thundered: 'Send more ammunition!'

Laughing, he removed the starched napkin he had kept tucked in his collar during the meal, neatly folded it and laid it next to his setting.

'Mind if I smoke?' he asked.

'Perhaps in the drawing room, dear,' Mary suggested, with understanding and tenderness.

Once there, Dooley offered Piccadilly Tipped from a chromium case.

'No? No takers?'

'Doctor Singleton and Roderick gave up tobacco some years ago,' Mrs Singleton busily explained. 'As an example to Mary, you understand.'

'Nice one. You thought she was going to start chewing it.'

Charles declined coffee, saying it would keep him awake all afternoon. All he wanted was to get out.

'I'll see you to your car, dear,' Mary said, when, not a second too soon, the time came.

'Wear something round your shoulders, dear,' Mrs Singleton trilled after her.

'I hope it wasn't too much of an ordeal,' Mary said, managing a smile as she pressed Dooley's hand. 'Father can be formidable, but the secret is to be formidable back.'

'I don't think there's going to be a return match,' Dooley answered, grimly.

And there wasn't.

Kitty said: 'D'you know what a gentleman is?'

'A bloke who gets out of the bath to relieve himself,' Dooley replied.

'It's a man who never knowingly embarrasses another person,' Kitty corrected, repeating with solemnity a favourite aphorism of her long-dead father. 'Would you say Doctor Singleton fits that description?'

'They weren't my sort of people, Kit. I was out of my depth.'

'And they watched you drown, didn't they? All except Mary. She had to let you go, didn't she?'

'I don't think she wanted to. We had a couple more dates, then she said she was sorry but an old flame had come back into her life and it wasn't fair to go on seeing me.'

Dooley could have added that Mary, on that last night in the Citroën, had kissed him as never before and had choked on sudden tears as she quickly left the car. She hadn't looked back. But the monumental conceit that made Dooley a difficult man to like was curiously absent where women were concerned. He couldn't believe he was attractive to them and so remained unconvinced by the clear evidence that Mary Singleton had been in love with him.

'Better finish your pint,' Kitty said, sympathetically. 'It's getting late.'

She felt sorry for him. She knew how it felt to have a wound that wouldn't heal.

He seemed not to have heard her last statement.

'I hadn't thought of marriage before Mary,' he mused, as if thinking aloud. 'Not seriously. Know what I mean?'

'Your landlady pampers you too much.'

'Well, that and being on the move all the time. Mary gave me an insight into what it could be like.'

'Careful, Sir Charles!' Kitty warned, laughing. 'I think you're about to fall off the shelf. Maybe all you need is a little encouragement.'

'Try me and prove me.'

'Your beer.'

'Mind if I leave it, Kit? Stomach's a bit humpty.'

'Where did you eat and what?'

'A seafood place in Liverpool.'

'Can I get you a glass of Andrews?'

'It'll pass. What do I owe you?'

'Nothing.'

Kitty didn't want her husband to know from the till roll that she and Dooley had stayed long enough together to have drinks.

'You'll come and see us again, won't you?' she asked, when the lounge was in darkness and they were standing face to face in the dim hall. 'We like your company.'

'I'll be back in January for the survey. That soon enough?'

'We'll be closed. Can't you come sooner? Where there's a will there's a way, Mr Dooley.'

'Charles.'

'Charles.'

'Leave it with me.'

'I'll see you in the morning. I'll be down before you leave.'

2

But he didn't go. On the Friday afternoon following his arrival, Frank explained to Gloria Raby that Chummy, as he called Dooley, was still in bed, awaiting a second visit from the Hatfields' doctor.

'Mild case of food poisoning,' he murmured, admiring the spectacular views from the twenty-second floor of Osprey Court through Gloria's powerful binoculars. 'New Leaf Hotel not guilty. He should be away in the morning, then we'll have the place to ourselves till Tuesday night, when the reps come back.'

'Sure you wouldn't like something stronger than orange juice, Frank?' Gloria asked. 'I've got most things short of paint remover.'

'Pity. That's all I drink nowadays. Juice will do fine, Gloria. Cath sends her apology for not coming today. Quite apart from Chummy's being taken bad, she'd made other arrangements that I didn't know about.'

'We'll catch up with each other. When the Lord made time, he made plenty of it. Excuse me for a moment.'

Scanning land and sea through the binoculars, Frank told himself that he would have difficulty in persuading his Cathy to visit Osprey Court despite her frequently expressed desire to see inside and even to live in one of its spacious and luxuriously appointed apartments. When he had mentioned that Gloria Raby hailed from the exclusive Mayfields suburb of Liverpool, she had said 'sounds more your sort than mine' and had promptly changed the subject, her unspoken fear being that the older woman might patronise her as the Singletons had patronised Charles.

'This incredible view must be more addictive than television,' Frank said, detecting Gloria's return.

'It's certainly more expensive.'

'There's the dear old New Leaf Hotel, nicely in focus and many times magnified. I see the retired couple are leaving us. The old boy spent his life weeding the main line from Lime Street to London Euston and now, having decorated everything in sight and got the garden the way the wife wants it, he's free to do whatever she likes.'

'You have a cynical view of marriage, though not as cynical as mine. Come and sit down.'

'Not cynical, just realistic. Hold hard a moment. I see our doctor parking his Wolseley behind Chummy's silver Citroën. Now with a bit of luck, Gloria, he'll declare our patient fit to return to active service. Won't that be nice?'

'How should I know when I've never met the man?'

'When did you come to live in Redstone Bay?' Frank asked, joining Gloria at the fireside.

'Mavis and I came here last Easter. Mavis de Lapp. She's the companion I mentioned when I was driving you home from the library on Wednesday. Here's your juice, dear. Mavis draws. She'll be somewhere on the promenade, sitting at her easel in a floppy hat and making the most of the sunshine after several days of grey skies. Cigarette? Sensible man. I get through a box a day, for God's sake, sometimes more if I can't sleep.'

'Have you tried giving up? There's not much we can't do in life if we really want to do it. I gave up when I was fourteen.'

'I gave up giving up when a friend told me that no sooner had she chucked it than she got pregnant.'

'Well, it doesn't seem to be doing you any harm. You're still the neat blonde with floury skin and dark blue eyes that I remember from my boyhood.'

'I still have pretty legs too. Don't look away. I like them to be admired. Mary Quant invented the mini skirt at my request. Not everyone knows that.'

Gloria crossed her legs with an unsettling hiss of nylon against nylon and slid her navy blue skirt yet further up her thighs.

'Aren't they lovely, Frank?' she teased. 'And they go right up to my bottom.'

From as early as her schooldays, she had enjoyed pretending to herself from time to time that she was a floozie asking for a light. She liked to dress the part at home in once-white court shoes, fishnet stockings, a saucy little skirt and a red silk blouse, low-cut and worn loose over the skirt.

She saw Frank swallow hard and was pleased.

'I'll make you glad you came alone this afternoon,' she promised, smiling and blowing smoke at the ceiling.

'Do I look sorry?'

'Look at my hands. They're like stars. Small and soft and very experienced. Little plump hands with dimples in the backs. Your mouth's gone dry, hasn't it? Wait till Mavis goes to the village. This is her coming now.'

She proved to be the opposite of Gloria in almost every respect. Gloria used to tell people that Mavis's blubber kept her warm while she sketched on the promenade. Mavis favoured voluminous floral dresses, bare legs, and mules that made a slip-slap sound as she walked. Her large face was freckled like her hands, her gingery hair dry and frizzy. Brown eyes with gold flecks in them were her most attractive feature. Big and bright, they became almost luminous with alarm when she spotted Frank. He saw them dart from him to Gloria and then to the two empty glasses on the long low box-frame table that stood in front of the softly hissing gas fire.

He rose, smiling, when Gloria introduced him. To his 'How d'you do', Mavis responded with a dismissive 'Hi' before asking Gloria if they were dining at home that evening.

'Yes. The two old sticks from downstairs are coming to play bridge. A fool of a game, to be sure, but it keeps me from shoplifting or growing cannabis in the window box. Are you going for the ice cream?'

'After I've tidied up.'

Mavis collected the glasses and Frank saw her sniff them as she slip-slapped to the open door and on into the kitchen.

Gloria started biting her nails.

She said: 'We hadn't been living here more than a couple of weeks, Mavis and I, when a pair of CID men turned up to ask me yet more questions about my poisonous husband.'

'Peter Raby,' said Frank. 'I never met him, but I used to hear about him from Bunny Littler when we lived at the same digs in Fox Hill.'

'They came into this room, all heavy and watchful and true to type, saw the view and forgot all about me. They made straight for the windows, where they took turns peering through my binoculars and exclaiming like schoolboys. Then they remembered what they'd come for and got all serious and frightening again.'

The interior of the apartment was no less impressive than the view over a calm sea to the horizon, gilded now by the first hint of sunset. So far, Frank had seen only the hall and the room in which they sat, which Gloria called her drawing room, but soon he was to see her lavender and ivory bedroom, complete with teddy bear, and later still a white and chromium bathroom clad and floored with glazed mulberry tiles.

Twice the size of the lounge-bar at the New Leaf Hotel, the drawing room was rectangular, closefitted with a Saxony carpet in plain pink wool, the wallpaper pale yellow with a pattern of gold fleurs de lys. All the woodwork had the silky glow and exquisite grain of Finnish birch. There were no books and no pictures. Bone china figurines stood on a wooden shelf over a gas fire that looked like an outsize mouth organ encased in copper, and above the shelf was an unusual diamond-shaped looking glass in a broad ebony frame. Red and yellow flowers filled copper bowls, table lamps with white shades complemented sconces and ceiling lights, and grey cushions lay on the long sofa and deep armchairs upholstered in the same burgundy velvet as the floor-length curtains. A Grundig cabinet television, a Bang & Olufsen record player and a Steinway grand completed the furnishings.

'Don't be fooled by Mozart's *Sonatas for Pianoforte*,' Gloria said, with a nod at the handsome volume, case-bound in sky blue with gold blocking that lay on the closed lid. 'I bought it when I decided to learn to play and before engaging a teacher. He took one look at it and grunted "You can forget that for at least five years" and started me off with some finger exercises. "When you can find middle C in the dark, I'll give you a simple tune to practise", he added.'

'And now you've found middle C and he's given you *Whispering*,' said Frank. 'I can see it on the rack.'

'It's me who's on the rack, being stretched to the limit of my sinews. I've just discovered there's a fresh horror called sight-reading and I'm expected to master it.'

'My practice piece as a boy was something called *Olaf the Dane* and I remember blundering through it on summer evenings when I should've been out with the lads, jeering after girls or stoning other youths. I finally gave up the struggle. My father wanted the best for me, Gloria. I wish he hadn't died while I was still fighting him. We'd have been pals later on. A lot of knowledge died with him: about the Western Front in the Great War, about early motor vehicles, largely handbuilt by the men who designed them, no two makes looking alike. What variety there was before mass production came along!'

'You'd have liked my parents' 1926 Bentley,' Gloria said, handing Frank the only photograph in the room. 'For reasons known only to himself, Daddy called it a Cricklewood Bentley.'

'Because the cars were made in Cricklewood until Bentley was taken over by Rolls-Royce and production moved to Derby and later Crewe. A Bentley built by Rolls-Royce is sometimes called a Crewe Bentley.'

'Fascinating!'

'Isn't it? I normally make a small charge for information of this kind, but as you're obviously a bit pushed . . . Are Mum and Dad still alive, Gloria?'

'Killed in a road accident.'

'A nice couple. They look as if they lived for each other.'

'They did. Which is why I'm glad they died together. Did you ever come to our house in Mayfields, Frankie?'

'No. Closest I ever got was a house called Khotan, just down the road from yours and owned by a couple named Dawpool. I remember that yours was called Ailsa. Dorothy used to talk about it and say she wished she lived there.'

'She used to say that to me too. We spent a lot of time together when we were both in our teens and early twenties and crazy about tennis and Bing Crosby. My parents were fond of your sister. I'll get you that cutting in a minute.'

Mavis appeared in the doorway, this time wearing black leather gloves and jingling keys on a ring, as Gloria replaced the photograph on its shelf next to her armchair.

'I'll take the BMW. The Humber's making that squealing sound again,' she announced. 'Okay?'

Gloria was biting one of her nails with the rapt determination of a dog gnawing a louse.

'Make an appointment to have it fixed on Monday,' she said, breaking off. 'We'll need the Humber for Preston. See you shortly, dear.'

She stood up and held out her hand to Frank, dimpled back uppermost, as though inviting him to kiss it.

'D'you like my rings?' she asked, childishly. 'One on each finger. Costume jewellery. I keep the real thing for special occasions.'

'I thought they were knuckledusters. Hadn't you better stop biting your nails while you've still got the stumps left?'

'If you'll excuse me, I'll find that newspaper for you now.'

Frank heard Mavis leave the flat as he walked to the window and picked up the binoculars. He was watching an Isle of Man boat bound for Liverpool when Gloria called to him from her bedroom.

'Can you help me, Frankie?'

He found her sitting on the edge of her vast, silk-encased bed, tugging at a drawer that she said was stuck.

'I need a big strong man,' she said, making room for Frank.

'Want me to fetch the hall porter?' he asked, sitting down.

She let her soft blond hair brush his cheek as he leant over her disturbing thighs. In the same moment, she pulled the drawer open.

It was empty.

'Silly me!' she chided herself. 'I'd have sworn the obituary was in here. Now I'll have to search for it and poor Frankie will have to come back again.'

Their lips met as they slipped into each other's arms. Gloria had scented herself, but had decided not to remove the rings.

'There isn't time today,' she murmured in Frank's ear. 'Can you manage tomorrow morning, darling, when dear Mavis goes to Fleetwood to shop for the weekend?'

The kissing continued, ever slower and deeper, until Gloria stopped and pushed her fingers through Frank's fair hair.

'You want me, don't you?' she stated rather than asked, in the dreamiest of faraway voices. 'The answer is in your greedy eyes and thumping heart.'

Frank swallowed hard.

'About eleven? It's my morning with our accountant.'

'Keep away from Cath. If you stand and deliver tonight, you won't be able to satisfy me. Be warned: I'm a maneater.'

Chapter Three

A family scene awaited him at the New Leaf Hotel. Sustained laughter from the lounge-bar met him in the hall. Inside the room, he found Kitty and Dooley seated one at each side of the log fire and Joyce's daughter, Isobel, running to and fro between their outstretched arms.

He stood for a moment in the doorway, watching merriment that made him feel annoyed and excluded.

'What's this?' he asked, coldly, when no one appeared to have noticed his arrival. 'Christmas morning?'

Isobel shrieked with joy as Dooley, with a cry of 'Gotcha!', pulled her onto his lap and started hugging and rocking her.

'How d'you like the lovely present we've just got from our patient?' Kitty asked her husband, nodding at the large bouquet that stood on one of the tables. 'You've been promoted. Read what it says on the label.'

She returned her mirthful attention to chuckling Isobel, wanting nothing so much as to kiss and cuddle her and tell her little stories.

'"To Doctor and Nurse Hatfield from Charles Dooley",' Frank read aloud and without enthusiasm. He paused, then: 'Thank you, Mr Dooley. Very kind.'

'No problem, young man,' Dooley responded, vigorously, tickling Isobel's chest and making her giggle and shrink from him. 'All part of the service.'

Kitty was walking towards the door now, her face rosy with lingering joy, her laughter dying as she passed Frank with the off-hand explanation that she was going to make some tea. It hurt him that she didn't ask what or who had delayed him.

He advanced slowly on Dooley.

'What did the MO have to say?' he asked, perching on the arm of Kitty's chair. 'Are you fit to return to the front line?'

'Ready to face shot and shell and fall for the flag if I must. I've enjoyed VIP treatment from you and your queen, young man. Haven't I, Isobel? It's been like staying at the Ritz only better.'

'We did nothing for you, Mr Dooley, that you wouldn't have done for us.'

'I call that civil.'

'All we did was call your office in London and your landlady in Birmingham. You ate next to nothing, so tonight you're our dinner guest.'

'Nice one. Nice one. And spoken in the nick of time, 'cos I was just about to eat Isobel. Hear that, my fairy?'

Isobel was lolling in the crook of Dooley's left arm, chuckling with glee while he made faces at her and stroked her bare thighs. Frank watched with distaste until his gaze moved to the half-emptied glass of beer at Dooley's elbow. He wondered how many pints the fellow had drunk since getting up.

'What time will you want breakfast in the morning?'

Dooley suggested nine o'clock. He was meeting Maurice Zerdin at the Blackpool store at ten for a belated inspection of the linoleum installation that Zerdin's had completed while he was laid low.

Frank said: 'Mr Zerdin lives along the coast at Vicker's Cross. I spotted his name in the telephone book one day and it brought back memories.'

'Lives at Bell House. Built to last for a Liverpool shipowner. They asked me to dinner there once – Maurice and his missis, Helen. Only she don't like me calling her Helen so I do it all the more 'cos she's got to take it from me on account of all the flooring work I put their way. The Coventry store took three thousand square yards of heavy lino. One store.'

'I hope he remembers you at Christmas.'

'Nah! Yours Truly don't take naffin from no one. A good lunch once in a while. That's all. I could've taken enough in bribes to build myself a mansion, but no thanks.'

Among those contractors wise enough to feed his gargantuan appetite, Charles was known as Pints Dooley. He brazenly chose the most expensive dishes in the most expensive restaurants and had no hesitation in calling for brandy and cigars if they weren't offered. Later, he would describe the feast in detail and with relish to his landlady, always concluding with 'Of course it was all properly served.' Dooley was very particular about correct procedure and quick to speak up if anything displeased him.

'Will you head straight for Birmingham after Blackpool or d'you spend your weekends in London?' Frank asked. 'My wife mentioned that your father still lives there.'

'Nah! I don't get down to The Smoke all that often. It's back to my Elsie. Back to Brum, Isobel, where the rustics say "Where yo go-een?"' Dooley declared, loudly. 'And who am I taking with me? Isobel!'

He let her down between his legs to the carpet; and it seemed to Frank, who was ready to think the worst of him, that he took the opportunity to maul her.

Her mother said pleasantly from the doorway: 'Only if you can promise her a good home, Mr Dooley.'

Frank stood up and walked towards her.

'Are you all right, Joyce?' he asked.

'I'm fine, Boss. It was only a filling.'

Joyce liked working at the hotel. She called her employers Boss and Missis despite the informality that Frank and Kitty would have preferred from one whom they treated as a friend. Frank wouldn't take any rent for the basement flat. 'It's only lying there doing nothing,' he said, after he and his Cathy had moved up to the attic. 'You and Isobel might as well have the use of it.'

'Sorry I'm late,' she said. 'The dentist had been called to the Cottage Hospital.'

She was down on one knee, straightening her daughter's dress, pushing stray hair from the child's brow and asking what she had done at school that afternoon.

'Auntie Kitty fetched you home, didn't she, sweetheart? You must say thank you when she comes back.'

As though on cue, Kitty came in bearing a tray laden with tea things.

'None for me, Cath,' Frank said. 'I'll have to change and get along to the Parish Hall. I've invited Mr Dooley to have dinner with us, so ask him what he'd like for the main course.'

'You're leaving early,' Kitty remarked. 'Your class isn't till six.'

'I should think keeping fit is all there is to do in Gravestone Bay at this time o' year, eh, Frank?' Dooley chirped, setting down his glass after draining it. 'Cor, what a boring place!'

'If you come again, I'll have the funfair opened for you,' Frank replied, coldly and without looking at him.

'Mummy, are we going to take Scamp for his walk?' Isobel asked her mother.

'Take your hat and coat off, Joyce, and sit down,' Kitty said. 'You'd like a cup of tea, I'm sure. And thanks for letting me have your little treasure this afternoon. I just wish she was mine.'

'I've already claimed her,' stated Dooley. 'Have your teeth drilled any time you like, Joyce. Hey, Frank! Before you go. Remind me to tell you a joke about dentists when the girls aren't around. Why is a dentist the luckiest geezer on earth? Think about it and I'll tell you later.'

'Give me your things, Joyce, and I'll put them on this chair,' Kitty said. Then, to her husband and with a hint of impatience: 'You've got time for a cuppa, surely?'

Dooley lowered his voice to a conspiratorial level.

'Kit! He's got a fancy woman somewhere,' he growled. 'What's the bettin' it's this Gloria bird you been tellin' me about, eh?'

Kitty blushed, averting her face from Frank, who was standing and looking on as if in the home of strangers, and said quickly that she wanted to hear about Osprey Court, likewise about Gloria Raby and Dorothy. Frank replied that he would have more to tell next day following a return visit to Gloria.

'She couldn't find the *Merseyside Express* with Penny

Bridge's article about my sister in it, so I'm going back in the morning. I'm anxious to read it.'

'Me too,' Kitty said. The squeak of amusement entered her voice when she added, smiling: 'I didn't know we had a celebrity in the family.'

Joyce said, sitting Isobel on her knee: 'I believe Osprey Court is the last word in luxury. Thick carpets in the corridors, basement garage, and a rooftop restaurant that only residents and their guests can use. A lady I know went there once for afternoon tea and she said it was like being in the Palm Court of Grand Hotel.'

Dooley draped his white handkerchief over his left shoulder and pretended he was bowing a violin.

'We take you now into the Bath Room at Pump,' he announced, 'where the Pandemonium Light Orchestra is already playing the Hosepipe from Handel's *Woh-er Music*.'

'I'll leave you to enjoy the concert,' Frank told his wife, without smiling.

On the stairs, as laughter subsided, he heard Dooley call for another pot of beer.

2

Only Charles Dooley and his hosts sat down to dinner that night. Following Jerusalem artichoke soup, Kitty brought in hot game pie in rich gravy, with carrots, peas, fried mushrooms and a tureen of steaming boiled potatoes.

'Have you ever thought of moving into the twentieth century, ole son, before it runs out?' Dooley asked Frank, mentally devouring the spread before physically attacking it. 'We've only got about thirty years of it left, remember, and an Englishman needs time.'

With a Hatfield to his left and right, he appeared to occupy the head of the four-seater table. His awareness of this, fortified by an afternoon of steady drinking and the knowledge that his companions were northerners, made him behave as though in charge of the proceedings.

'Your queen tells me you died in 1950,' he continued, watching Frank open a bottle of Mouton Cadet.

'It's only what you tell people yourself, Frank,' Kitty said, innocently, but with imps in her eyes that her husband didn't see. 'You say it with that nice smile of yours and it makes them laugh.'

'I'm concerned about you, young man, because you're living in a fur-lined rut,' Dooley stated, emboldened by Kitty's sly amusement. 'By the time I was your age, I'd been three times round the world. Where've you been? – apart from Andover when you was a Brylcreem Boy.'

'Mr Dooley asked me about your National Service and I said you'd done it in the air force,' Kitty explained, promptly. 'I hope I got that right.'

Dooley had served in the REME.

'Know what that stands for?' he asked his host. 'Royal Electrical and Mechanical Engineers. Second World War. I was one of the first Brits into Paris in 1944 and from there I went all over Germany. With the end of the war, I became the only service engineer on the payroll of the Baldwin Electric Car Company, and that had me flying to any place in the world where a Baldwin car was in trouble. I don't expect you or anyone else in Gravestone Bay have heard of the Baldwin.'

Kitty laughed and warned Dooley to watch out because 'Frank has loads of picture books about old cars and buses and if anyone's heard of the Baldwin it'll be Frank.'

Both men smiled at her, thinking how attractive she looked in the pearl grey two-piece that Frank liked her to wear. Her blouse was pink with a ruffled front and collar and her red lipstick matched her painted nails and high heeled shoes. Because it suited her slender face, her hairstyle had remained the same since her late teens. Called the feather cut, it consisted of a flat crown within a wreath of four-inch curls.

Frank said: 'The Baldwin was as far ahead of its time as the Q type AEC bus, which is probably why neither of them were in production for long.'

'See!' cried Kitty, all but thrusting her tongue out at Dooley.

'Four years,' he replied, with his mouth full of dinner, his elbows out and his napkin tucked into his shirt collar. 'Jack

Baldwin was the sort of bloke who can go bust without noticing it. Mechanical genius, sure: businessman, never. If he'd got himself a proper accountant instead of leaving the pounds shillings and pence to his scatter-brained wife, he'd be in business to this day.'

'I'm not so sure, but we won't fall out over it. Will you have a glass of wine with us?'

'No, thank you, young man. Yours Truly'll stick to beer, if it's all the same to you.'

'Please yourself. You're the guest.'

'And you're the mystery man. Not even your queen can tell me what makes you tick,' Dooley declared, settling contentedly to his subject. 'You don't watch telly, you don't go to the pictures, you don't follow football any more. What's left?'

Annoyed, Frank looked quickly at his wife. She didn't look at him.

'Books,' said Dooley, in answer to his own question. 'Hitler burned them. Only sensible thing that geezer ever done. Know the best job for you, Frank? Schoolmaster. Old style. Black gown and a mortar board. I can just see you standing in front of the class with a book in your hands reading aloud to the boys. Can't you, Kit? It's the voice. You sound like a parson doing a burial service. I'll 'ave some more o' that red cabbage.'

'Frank can't help the way he speaks,' Kitty said, with neither approval nor disapproval. 'He went to a public school, where he was taught to speak proper. Not like me.'

Dooley guffawed.

'Nor me. What did they teach you there, Frank?' he asked.

'Same as they teach at any other school.'

Kitty said: 'Now you're being modest.'

'Latin? Shakespeare?' Dooley jeered. 'If you went to a public school, ole son, why aren't you a doctor or a lawyer or something worthwhile? What are you doing in Gravestone Bay, bowing and scraping to a bunch of reps in Hepworth suits? It don't make sense.'

Dooley paused, watching his prey, feigning puzzlement. Heavy with food and drink, reminding Frank of a grossly inflated toad, he was enjoying his moment, making sport of the man of whom he was jealous as the Singletons had made sport of him.

'I'll fetch the dessert,' Kitty said, quietly.

'Someone's got to keep the home fires burning,' she heard her husband say as she left the room. 'I see nothing wrong with the life we lead here and neither does my wife. If she does, she's never said so.'

'Know why? Because she's never known nothing different, any more than you have. Kit's still alive, but not for much longer if she stays in a place where everything closes except the public toilets for six months out of every twelve.'

Dooley mopped up what remained of his gravy with a piece of buttered bread before setting the empty plate aside to make room for the dessert.

'How often d'you come to this part of the world, Mr Dooley?' Frank asked, dabbing his lips with his napkin.

He looked up, startled, when Dooley farted.

'As often as I choose,' the man replied, slowly.

For a moment they stared at one another in silence. Frank's eyes were aflame with disgust, Dooley's steady and unashamed.

Returning, Kitty said: 'It's fruit salad, boys, with vanilla ice cream. Hope you'll like it.'

'Like anything you do,' Dooley said, smiling as he watched her regain her seat. Then, having drained his glass tankard: 'After this, we're off to Blackpool. I'm treating both of you to a night club. I want Frank to see the inside of one while he can still get about.'

'Ah, that was unkind!' Kitty protested, mildly.

'I'll live to dance on *your* grave,' Frank told Dooley, with a nod at the older man's belly. 'We appreciate your offer, but the clubs are all closed at this end of the year.'

'They'll be open this week for the lights,' Kitty said. 'We could lock up here, Frank, and go for an hour or so. It's Saturday tomorrow. We could leave the cash-and-carry till Monday.'

'With respect to Mr Dooley, I don't think he's in any condition to drive a car.'

'Taxi there, taxi back. All included in the treat,' cried

Dooley. 'You'd like to go, Kit, I can tell. So all we need do now is persuade the parson here. I don't expect you've ever been to see the lights, have you, ole son?'

'Another time perhaps, Mr Dooley,' Frank answered. 'You've already been very kind to us.'

'Oh, eh! Isn't he smooth, Kit? Isn't he cool?' Dooley demanded, leering contemptuously at his host. 'What do I have to do to bring him to life? Just tell me.'

'I think he's right about the club. Blackpool will be choked with traffic tonight. By the time we found somewhere, it'd be time to come back.'

Frank rose.

'If you'll excuse me now, I've got a session with our accountant tomorrow and I'll have to get some figures together before bed.'

'So if I smell burning in the night, it's the books,' roared Dooley.

'Will you clear up, Cath, and see if there's anything Mr Dooley would like to take up to his room before you close the bar?'

'Yours Truly will settle for anything in a skirt,' Dooley called after his host. 'Sleep tight, young man, and don't take life too seriously. You'll never get out of it alive.'

Frank was at his desk in the tiny office under the stairs when Kitty joined him ten minutes later and softly closed the door.

Dooley had gone to bed.

'You forgot to give him my blood group and my inside leg measurement,' Frank stated, grimly, and without looking up from his calculations. 'What went wrong? Did you run out of time?'

'I had to talk about something when I took things to his room or when he was sitting on his own in the lounge. He asked questions and what could I do except answer them?'

'Who said he could call you Kit?'

'Nobody.'

'Were you drinking with him while I was at the Parish Hall?'

'Of course not!' Kitty lied, indignantly. 'Why should I want to drink with him?'

'He's not to come here again. Tell Joyce. We're permanently full. You give him his breakfast in the morning and see him off the premises. Is that clear?'

'That's clear.'

'I'll never allow that man under my roof again.'

Kitty, standing behind her husband, placed her hands on his shoulders and kissed the top of his head.

'I'm sorry, Frank,' she said, softly. 'But what could I do?'

Frank didn't answer.

3

Gloria draped herself round his neck the moment they were together behind her front door.

'Darling, you're so late!' she complained. 'It's turned twelve o'clock.'

'Sorry! The meeting with Simon took longer than expected.'

'Simon?'

'Our accountant. I've made quite a decision.'

The couple walked hand in hand into the drawing room, Gloria deliberately stopping on a spot from which Frank could enjoy a back view of her naughty skirt and high heels reflected in the looking glass above the fire place. Her arms encircled his neck again as she raised one knee and slid her thigh between his legs.

'Ready for bed?' she murmured. 'I'll give you such a lovely time, Frankie.'

One kiss became two, then three, then four; and they were eye-closing, tongue-stretching kisses such as Frank had not experienced in a long time. He needed all his resolve to say: 'I can't. Not this morning.'

'Why? What's the matter?' Gloria crooned, gently rubbing her nose against his ear. 'Have you been disobedient? Were you up and coming last night after I'd forbidden it?'

'It isn't that. Cath and I hardly bother these days.'

Slowly and reluctantly, Frank released himself from Gloria's hold and smiled down at her pouty face.

'We're having an early lunch because Cath's going with our helper and her little girl to a children's party,' he lied.

'They're taking cakes and jellies and so on. I'd forgotten about it.'

'I'll forgive you this once,' Gloria sighed, letting go of Frank's hands. 'Anyhow, we'll have Mavis back shortly.'

'I don't think she likes me.'

'It isn't dislike. She's wary of everyone who comes here. One day I'll tell you why, but now we're going to have some coffee and you're going to tell me about the decision you made when you were with Simon. Sit down on the sofa in front of the nice warm fire and read about your famous sister.'

While Gloria went through to her kitchen, Frank picked up the paper she had indicated. He located Dorothy's obituary, but his thoughts kept straying to his Cathy while he was trying to read it. He wanted to be alone with her, to put his arm round her narrow shoulders and kiss her pretty nose and dew-wet mouth and call her Cathy because he loved her name and tell her of his newly-formed plans, plans that outlawed such thoughts as he had had of being unfaithful to her.

Gloria returned, closing the door with her foot.

'I considered slipping Spanish fly into your coffee, which would've had you stalking dogs on your way home; but instead, because you've let me down, I've added a lethal dose of laxative.'

'My pal,' murmured Frank, laying aside the *Merseyside Express*. 'Now I'll be able to enjoy a seat in the circle without buying a ticket.'

Gloria said: 'I'm determined to seduce you, Frankie dear, because I'm curious to find out what you're like in bed.'

She placed the coffee things on the low table that stood between the fire and the sofa, sat down with her warm thigh against Frank's and filled their cups.

'You may need coaching,' she decided, eyeing critically his Lovat suit, his check shirt, his knitted tie, his buff waistcoat and brown suede shoes. 'From what I've seen of you so far, you're rather dull, rather conventional. Bourgeois.'

She asked if Cath ever did 'something special' for him, giving it its number, which struck Frank as bourgeois coming from a woman who was in most respects bohemian.

He shook his head.

'She says it's dirty.'
'Did your first wife?'
'Clare kept it as a treat.'
'She was a manipulator.'
'Aren't all women?'
'Men are beasts, Frankie darling, and have to be tamed. A clever woman can do it without showing him the whip.'
'The whip meaning nagging.'
'That's the obvious way; but there are others, better and more subtle, such as flattery, plying him with the food he likes or keeping sex as a reward for good behaviour. A nagging wife, if you want my opinion, is a stupid wife. Instead of cultivating her wiles, especially her sweetness, she nags more and more as she becomes less and less attractive. I sometimes wonder if women, whether naggers or not, who live with men without the marriage tie, realise the risk they run of being abandoned when they're past their best. Men don't grow old, remember. Women do.'
'How did you control Raby?'
'I didn't. Couldn't. Ours wasn't a standard marriage. He lived in my house, but he wasn't dependent on me for a clean shirt and something to eat. We both had money. Mine came from my kinsfolk, his from whoever wasn't looking.'
Frank was smiling.
'He was a womaniser,' he said. 'Bunny Littler used to tell me about him when he dropped in for a cup of tea at the gymnasium I had in Liverpool.'
'Raby couldn't keep his flies fastened. You've heard of Camelot? Well, he was known to his drivers, Bunny included, as Cumalot. Bed was all that united us. We took holidays together, lived well, socialised occasionally; but mostly we lived separate lives. I suppose I was nuts to marry him, but I like a man about the house. Your sister identified him as a rogue in two seconds, young though she was, and my mother eventually barred him from Ailsa.'
Frank's smile had broadened.
He said: 'I remember reading in the *Express* about his garage in Coxside going up in flames and half a dozen of his hire cars with it. Bunny once told me that Raby used to say,

whenever he saw the fire brigade dashing to a fire, "There they go – the interfering bastards".'

'It was the blaze that finally brought the police to our door. I was in hospital recovering from a nervous breakdown when he jumped bail and cleared off with my housekeeper, my Bentley Continental and all things prized and portable. The sod would've taken my Steinway if he could have got it on his back. Talking of thieves, you stole a glance at your watch just then, young man.'

'Don't call me that, Glorious,' Frank said, quietly. 'I don't like it.'

He put his arm round Gloria's shoulders as she turned to face him with a question in her eyes.

They kissed.

'I'll have to go'

'You'll come back.'

'With the paper. But I don't know when. I want my Cathy to read it.'

'What's she like, your Cathy? D'you carry a photo of her? Is she a modern woman? That tensed you up, Frank. Why?'

'Just passing thoughts. D'you believe a change of scene could affect a woman's fertility?'

'Oh my! What a question! I'd say it's possible. Are you thinking of Cath? I haven't asked you if you have any children, have I? I just somehow concluded you hadn't.'

'I'm thinking we might move back to Liverpool. That's what I've been discussing with Simon, who's our financial adviser as well as our accountant. I may put a manager into the hotel.'

Gloria, bending forward from her seat on the sofa, was lighting one of her Fribourg & Treyer cigarettes with a heavy table lighter.

She asked what he would do in Liverpool.

'I may not do anything at first. Top priority is a proper holiday for both of us. We normally decorate while the hotel is closed, but this time I'm going to take Cath wherever she fancies going. I may even buy a car and learn to drive.'

'And what, pray, has caused this minor revolution? It all sounds fresh from creation.'

‘I’ve been thinking about it on and off for some time,’ Frank answered, convincingly. ‘If we’re to have a family, we’ve got to get cracking now. Cath won’t foster and she won’t adopt. Variety, a change of air, a more normal way of life – these may just do the trick. Anyhow, it’s worth a try, isn’t it?’

He was too late.

Chapter Four

A tearful and baffled Joyce handed him a sealed note on his return to the New Leaf Hotel. As he tore it open, certain of what he would find, she explained that Dooley had come back from Blackpool around twelve noon, had brushed her aside and gone straight up to the attic flat. Not two minutes later, he had come down again, a suitcase in each hand and 'the Missis', dressed for the street, hard on his heels. Before Joyce could gather her wits, she had been kissed on the cheek, bade goodbye and left gaping on the top step as the lovers sped away.

'What are we going to do, Boss?' she wailed.

'Nothing,' Frank muttered, in abject defeat. 'The note makes that all too clear.'

He read it aloud to Kitty's mother early in December, sitting in the gloomy and depressing living room of her home in the Waverton district of Liverpool.

I feel such a coward, Frank, doing it this way, but it's easier for both of us than face to face and it amounts to the same thing. I thank you with all my heart for the years we've spent together and wish you the happiness you deserve. All I'm taking with me and all I want is the jewellery you gave me every year on my birthday and that I'll always keep. Goodbye, dear Frank, and thanks. Cath.

'She rang me up from Birmingham the day she left you,' Mrs Osborne said, from the depths of her broken-down armchair.

She sighed. Then, in a weary voice and gently massaging her brow with her fingertips: 'Well, you know that without me reminding you, of course you do, because I rang you the same day, or was it the day after? I forget. The days run into each other when you're retired and on your own with nothing to do except read and think. It was different when I had the flower shop. I can only say, Frank,' she concluded, heaving her voice to a higher register, 'that I think she's out of her mind, leaving you for this Dooley or whatever his name is.'

'Has Cath phoned you since, Mum?'

'She rings me every Friday, Frank, same as she did from Redstone Bay.'

'How does she sound? Happy?'

'Well, you know Cath, Frank. She's always bright, so it's hard to tell how she really feels. At the moment, it's Charles this and Charles that, but he's still a novelty, isn't he?'

'Have you met him yet?'

'Frank, the man hasn't even had the courtesy to say hello over the telephone. They're coming here for Christmas and New Year. I suppose I'll have to be polite with him for Cath's sake.'

'I had a feeling they'd come, which is why I decided to bring you your present now. As you know, Cath and I always had Christmas dinner with Clare and Nick Pound before coming here for the evening. Cath and Dooley might keep up the tradition. I'll probably spend Christmas in London with a lady friend.'

'Oh, I'm glad you've got someone. Is she nice, Frank?'

'She's given me a lot of support. I needed it at first. Ask Cath, will you, if she knows if Clare and Nick have sold the gymnasium? There was talk of it.'

'Your old place? Peterkin's? No. Clare and Nick have bought a house in Ringwood because the living quarters at Peterkin's were too cramped now that the twins are getting bigger. Someone called Farr, I think Cath said, has moved into the flat over the gym.'

'Varr. Willie Varr. He was one of my assistants. Nick Pound was another, of course.'

'What will you do now, Frank?'

'Sell the hotel and see what's happening outside Redstone Bay. If I'd had the sense to do that six months ago, I might still have Cath.'

'Would you take her back if she asked you to?'

Frank didn't answer.

'Nothing would please me more than to see you together again,' Mrs Osborne admitted.

But her desire for a reconciliation was not shared by her daughter. Kitty was happier with Charles Dooley than ever she'd been with Frank Hatfield, although at first she had feared the future as much as Frank had regretted the past.

She had cried for most of the journey to Birmingham, but her cheeks were dry and freshly powdered by the time Dooley drove the Cit into the car park of the small hotel in Hadley Road where they would stay while seeking a flat for themselves and a job for Kitty. But her tears returned at bedtime, following a copious dinner and too much vodka, sparked by the spectacle of naked Dooley leering at her from the bathroom doorway.

'The flesh lusteth, Kitty,' he growled, savouring the words.

Perched on the edge of the double bed, ready but anxious in lace-trimmed satin, Kitty cringed as he crept up on her like a stage villain, licking his chops and flicking his genitals at her.

'The flesh lusteth,' he repeated.

Kitty shrank from his bear-like body, covering her wet eyes with both hands so as not to see his heavy brown cluster and the great belly with a navel like a child's ear.

'Is this all you want me for?' she sobbed.

She yelped as he ripped her nightdress from bodice to hem, then found herself trapped under his weight, wide-eyed and trembling.

'This and lots more,' he chortled. 'You're going to run round the room with nothing on. You'll dance on a sixpence if that's what I want.'

'You're raping me,' Kitty gasped.

'Nice one. Nice one. But there's a difference. You're going to love it. So wrap your little fist round this, my queen, and start rubbing. Have fun. Let it happen.'

'This is what's known as paying for the meal,' Kitty moaned, before Dooley had begun to stimulate her.

'You're only just starting to pay. Uncle Charles has a lot of surprises in store for this little monkey.'

Kitty was soon to realise that Dooley's huge appetite was not restricted to food and Reklaw's bitter. She was also to discover his penchant for walking about their flat stark naked. 'Ever ready,' he would say, cuddling her while she was preparing a meal or making their bed. 'Ever ready.'

He snored heavily that first night while Kitty lay sleepless and unsatisfied at his side, resolved to telephone Frank and ask if he would take her back. But Sunday was dry and sunny and even warm to one accustomed to seaside temperatures. After a nourishing breakfast, the couple set off in the Cit to meet Elsie ('You've picked a rum one,' she told Kitty, laughing, while Dooley was packing in his room) and then to start looking for somewhere to live. At the end of a day in which she noticed how generous Dooley was, Kitty went calmly to bed and Frank was forgotten. Except between the sheets, where he was rough and selfish, Charles was very considerate of her.

Next morning, drying her black curls as she came out of the bathroom, Kitty found him standing naked at the window of their room, looking out over the Monday morning traffic making its way nose-to-tail along Hadley Road into central Birmingham.

She tiptoed up behind him and covered his eyes with her hands.

'Oh no you don't, Charles Dooley,' she told him, firmly. 'I know who you're watching for. Mary Singleton.'

He turned round, grinning, and put a fist like a pound of sausages under Kitty's nose.

'D'you want it? D'you want it?' he asked, pleasantly. 'Speak to me like that again and you'll wake up on the other side of the room. Get our laundry together and take the sack to reception before nine o'clock.'

Within a week, Mrs Osborne told Frank, the couple had found a self-contained flat, and Kitty, exploring Birmingham on foot while Charles was gone about his business, had got herself a job in a dry cleaner's shop. Her mother admitted this with a certain grudging, neglecting to add that, thanks to

Dooley's spotting the advertisement and urging his queen to apply, Kitty was to start work after Christmas as a teacher in a catering college.

'Have you thought of asking her to come back to you, Frank?' Mrs Osborne coaxed.

'I've certainly thought of it, Mum, of course I have. But there doesn't seem much point in asking now, does there? Not after what you've been telling me.'

2

'This is it,' Gloria said, having stopped her BMW close to a corner shop in a Preston backstreet.

'This is what?' Frank asked.

Gloria was looking at the front door that gave access to the flat above the shop.

'Home of the Preston Hotshots,' she explained. 'Come and I'll show you. It'll give us something to talk about on the drive to London. I managed to bag us a suite at Brown's Hotel, Frankie dear, right through till the first week in January. That should give us plenty of time to talk to Dorothy's publisher. Is there a dinner suit in your case?'

'I can hire one in London.'

'Hire one, my foot!' Gloria snorted. 'We'll go to Savile Row this afternoon and on from there if they've nothing off the peg.'

She opened the door to the flat and Frank followed her upstairs. At any other time, he would have been aroused by her shapely legs in seamed nylons, her snake skin court shoes and tight little black skirt beneath a red silk blouse; but she had given him a busy night.

'Have you brought something to go with my dinner suit?' he asked, when they paused for a moment at the top of the stairs. 'I don't want to feel ashamed of you.'

She returned his smile, saying she had packed a bronze silk cocktail dress to complement her blue eyes, golden hair and chalk-white skin.

'You'll like it,' she predicted. 'When you come to live with me and we have evenings at the Ninian and suchlike, you'll discover that I have some exquisite clothes. Twenty years ago, when we were girls together, Dorothy used to castigate me for dressing like a gangster's moll when I had a wardrobe full of best clothes. Little did I realise then that I'd one day marry a gangster. Go through to the parlour, Frankie darling, while I fix some Camp coffee for us. Switch the electric fire on, will you?'

'Place smells damp.'

'I haven't used it since you and I became chums,' Gloria called from the kitchen. 'I'll probably ask a local estate agent to find me a tenant. Anything new with the New Leaf Hotel?'

'Simon thinks he's got a buyer - a retired policeman, still under fifty, and his wife. It's as well to get rid of it now, don't you think? The steam train created the seaside holiday and its demise will soon be felt by the guest houses. Sundown and Sea Breezes'll be converted into bedsits. Besides, it's cheaper now to take the family abroad.'

It was a neat little flat, if a trifle dark. On his way to the parlour, Frank had passed a combined lavatory and bathroom and glimpsed a bedroom with little in it save a double bed ready for use. The focal point of the parlour was a cast iron fireplace, its starkness relieved by a column of green tiles at each side of a grate sealed with hardboard. The furniture was basic and well-used, like that in Mrs Osborne's living room, comprising a plain oatmeal haircord carpet with Congoleum surrounds, a bare table with three bentwood chairs tucked under it, a Rexine-covered sofa and two fireside chairs. An oblong coffee table stood in front of a two-bar Belling electric fire. The clock on the mantelpiece had stopped.

'How long did your gangster get?' Frank asked, 'if it isn't too personal a question.'

'Nothing's too personal for me. Here's your coffee. Help yourself to sugar and milk powder. Raby's due out next year. He's in Strangeways.'

'D'you visit him ever?'

'Are you crazy? After what he did to me? I'm just a little fearful the sod might visit me - or try to. That's why I'm living in Redstone Bay instead of Liverpool. That's why my number's ex-directory.'

'Was this flat his? You've told me he slept around.'

'No. I bought it after he went to prison. Can you guess what goes on within these four walls?'

'You chair discussion groups.'

Gloria sat down and lit a cigarette.

'I bring teenage boys here. Mavis and I pick them up in the clubs. She plays her trombone in here while I entertain in the bedroom. If there are two, one stays with her till my red light comes on. Mavis herself doesn't indulge. Anyhow, the boys don't fancy her. All that blubber . . .'

'Are you kidding me? I'm never sure when to take you seriously.'

'That's because I tell lies. Can't help it. But not this time. Don't forget your coffee. I stick with youths because men are dangerous – or can be. Don't look so suburban, dear. Fact is I can't do without the cock.'

'Now I *know* you're kidding.'

'If I try to deny myself, I become depressed to the point where I can think of nothing else.'

'Aren't you afraid of catching a dose?'

'I'm careful whom I pick – clean-looking boys with open faces and caring mothers. Oh, they're lovely at that age! They have flat stomachs, their hair smells of sea salt and they shoot high and hot. Only snag is they come too easily.'

'Do I?'

'You're improving. And me? Am I helping you to forget Cath?'

'I'm surprised, even ashamed, at the way I'm getting over it.'

'That's because you fell into the arms of a woman who can make you take off without wings. And,' said Gloria, looking at the tiny gold watch that was always slipping round her wrist, 'I suggest we take off ourselves about now. Oh, and we mustn't forget to call at Sweetens and see if they have any of Dorothy's novels in stock. Ready?'

Once on the road, Frank noticed again Gloria's driving skill. She was completely relaxed and in control, being accurate in her manoeuvres, reacting calmly and immediately to changing conditions and sometimes even anticipating them.

'The clown in front is about to do something stupid. I can tell the way he's shaping,' she would say; and almost always she was right. No: her car didn't have automatic transmission.

'With a manual box, you've got your vehicle by the throat,' she maintained. 'That matters when there's ice and slush on the roads. I use the gears rather than the brakes for controlling my speed. Believe it or not, I can get seventy thousand miles out of a set of tyres and still have an unused spare.'

Her BMW saloon was the 3200 CS, white with blue hide upholstery, and it floated along, at first through city traffic and then in the fast lane of the M6. Gloria drove in stockinged feet, wearing sun glasses and with a cigarette between her lips or fingers.

She glanced sideways at Frank, who had read again Penny Bridge's obituary notice of his sister and was now leafing through *Spring Term at Walker's Croft* by Mary Orchard.

'Sweetens' manager found it tucked away in his stock room and came out smiling and blowing the dust off it,' Frank said.

'That's why you were so long! I thought maybe you'd joined the Preston Light Infantry.'

'I wonder why Dorothy wrote under the name of Mary Orchard. According to the obituary, her married name was Blanchard.'

'Your sister was a very secretive person, Frank. Surely you noticed?'

'All her novels are out of print, so how am I going to read them all?'

'Don't ask me. Ask yourself if it's worth your while writing her biography.'

'I must have something to do. It's not enough for me to just loll around and play bridge with two old maids who swoon at sight of a raised lavatory seat. Besides, digging into Dorothy's past might be fun. For example, there's this secretary of hers . . . Ida Prince. Penny Bridge hints there may have been something between them.'

Gloria stiffened, and held her breath for a moment. Then: 'How can you say that about your own sister?' she asked, looking directly ahead.

'Now who's being suburban?'

'Dorothy was a married woman,' Gloria said, quietly and conclusively.

'Is that always a guarantee?'

'I believe so. What makes you think you're capable of writing a biography? Writers are normally lawyers or doctors or academics.'

'I doubt if the authors of the sort of books you read fall into any of those categories.'

'What I read is only fireside fiction. I meant literature. Biography. Social history. The stuff you read.'

'Maybe you're right and maybe not. Let's hear what Dorothy's publishers have to say, now that we know who they are,' Frank said, opening the novel again. He read aloud: 'Marjorie d'Or Adventure Library, Hoseside, London, EC 1.'

'We can phone them from Brown's and fix an appointment to see someone in authority. Unless you'd rather go alone.'

'Alone? Why alone? You haven't changed your mind, have you, about being my unpaid secretary and research assistant? If we're lucky, Marjorie d'Or may still have a few of Dorothy's titles in their warehouse. If we're luckier still, they might show an interest in the biography and offer to publish it.'

3

As he and Gloria stepped into the Nolans' house in the fashionable London suburb of Norris Green, Frank said: 'We won't stay long, Mrs Nolan,' and Gloria added: 'It's very kind of Mr Nolan to see us.'

'Mark's looking forward to meeting you,' Sarah Nolan assured them. Holding on to the front door before closing it, she suddenly laughed, gave a little leap backwards and choked out the words: 'He's been given three months to live, so . . .'

While Frank and Gloria stared after her in alarm, she led the way through the house, talking nervously about the weather, and into a heated conservatory floored with cardinal red quarry tiles and furnished with pink wicker chairs that would have been more at home in a bedroom. A matching table stood among them, its top covered with a sheet of clear glass held in place by brass corners.

Mark Nolan greeted the visitors from a reclining chair placed within arm's length of an electric radiator. He shook hands and managed a smile when apologising for not getting up. As though in his stead, a black and white collie, young and playful, rose from a raffia mat at his side and came to sniff delicately at Frank and then at Gloria as they took their seats. Satisfied of their good intentions, he returned to his mat and started gnawing one paw.

'That's our Sam,' Sarah explained, watching him with a smile. 'He's very loving. Like my husband. Are you all right, dear?'

A moment later, she excused herself with the comment that she had never met Dorothy and so couldn't answer questions about her.

'But Mark, as you've already discovered, was her agent for ten years. In fact, he got her started on her career as Mary Orchard.'

'I don't recall Dorothy's ever mentioning that she had a brother, Mr Hatfield,' Mark said, in a voice saddened and enfeebled by the cancer that was killing him. 'She never spoke of her family. You were given my name by her publisher, Sarah tells me. I'm sorry I couldn't come to the telephone myself. Not too stuffy for you in here, I hope? I have a job keeping warm these days.

He was a very different Mark Nolan from the brisk and enterprising West Ender whom Dorothy had liked and respected. The flat brown eyes, crinkly hair, yellowish skin and thick Ashkenazi nose and lips were unchanged, as were the discoloured teeth with many gold fillings; but Mark had lost a lot of weight, and the check suit, silk shirt and colourful bow tie that had once distinguished him had given way to a soft shirt open at the throat and a cable stitch pullover. His lower half was wrapped in a steamer rug.

Frank explained that Dorothy's publishers, so far from being helpful, had been downright hostile. After explaining his kinship and purpose, he had finally got through to the editorial director, who had snapped: 'What is the inquiry? You've got me out of an important meeting. Mary Orchard? Mary Orchard is dead and her name has been removed from our list. What? I have no idea where she lived. I'm putting you back to my secretary and she'll give you the name and address of her agent, who may be able to help you.'

'I know who that was,' Mark said, ruefully. 'Muriel Lint. She didn't like Dorothy and she resented my closeness to her predecessor in the editorial chair, Eddie Lombard. A nasty piece of work.'

Frank said: 'Her manner threw me completely. It was so unexpected. She hung up even before I had a chance to ask if she knew where I might find copies of my sister's books.'

'The remainder shops in Charing Cross Road are your best bet, I should think.'

'We tried them all this morning, Mr Nolan,' Gloria said, in a bored voice. 'My legs are reduced to stumps. Sam would've liked all that walking, wouldn't you, Sam?' she continued, bringing the collie to her side with his tail wagging. He moved in closer when she started tickling his ears. 'Oh, you're all for that, aren't you, Sam?'

Mark was smiling at him affectionately.

'He sits with me most of the day. Our younger daughter – the one who's still at home – takes him to the park in the morning and again before dinner.'

'You're straight out of Walt Disney, Sam,' Gloria declared. Then: 'Oh, I love dogs! We always had one at home and after I married I had two beautiful Afghan hounds. Snips and Snaps. They were my children, Mr Nolan, but other homes had to be found for them when I moved to my present address, where pets aren't allowed.'

During her several weeks in Liverpool's Elderfield Private Hospital, the dogs had been boarded in a kennels, put there by Peter Raby before his flight to the Channel Islands, where he was eventually rearrested and brought back to the mainland to face trial. At Brown's Hotel, in an exchange of confidences, Frank had revealed that his wife (he no longer thought of her as his Cathy) wanted a divorce, and Gloria admitted having lied to conceal the true reason for her incarceration in Elderfield. 'It wasn't a nervous breakdown. I'd become an alcoholic. I was getting through a bottle of Gordon's a day.'

'Because of Raby?'

'No. I didn't give a hoot about Raby. Boredom. I've never had a job that lasted more than a few days, never had an aim in life. I drifted into sex, drifted into marriage, drifted into the drying room at Elderfield. My minder there was Mavis de Lapp. You wondered why Mavis was wary of you at first. Well, now you know. She's my companion and also my bottle-watcher. Mavis knows how easily I could be coaxed into the cellar, so all visitors are kept under surveillance. When my time was up at Elderfield, I persuaded her with a fat salary and a new Humber Estate to move in with me.'

'Why Redstone Bay?'

'Because it's Mavis's home town and a place where Raby is unlikely to look. Osprey Court, in case you haven't noticed, is tightly guarded. A lot of money lives in Osprey Court.'

Frank was thinking how well the silence, the isolation and the opulence of 'Millionaire Mansions' would have suited Dorothy when Mark asked if he had tried Foyle's for copies of her novels.

He had.

'The assistant we spoke to had never heard of Mary Orchard. I gather she shot up like a rocket and fell to earth just as quickly. Did she make a lot of money from her books, Mr Nolan?'

'She had no cause for complaint. I wasn't just your sister's literary agent, Mr Hatfield: I had the privilege of being someone she trusted with the management of her affairs. I found the Willow Square house for her. She let me choose her car. We were friends, Dilly and I. Dilly was what her husband called her. It began as Daffodil, then got shortened.'

Frank was writing in a notebook resting on his knee.

'Her husband was Robin Blanchard. Am I right?' he asked. 'And she had a secretary named Ida Prince.'

'Sarah said you're staying at Brown's Hotel. Look across Albemarle Street and you'll see Blanchard Brothers' showroom. Bespoke gun makers. Robin was the son of Max Blanchard, who, with his brother, ran the company. Max and Robin never saw eye-to-eye. As soon as he was old enough, Robin got a job as a window dresser in one of the Oxford Street department stores and took a basement flat near the

BBC. He married Dorothy and they lived there till the move to Willow Square - number 38 - not far from Harrods.'

Gloria asked, still making much of Sam, if there were any children.

'No. I think Dilly told me she had a still birth at some time. Robin, of course, had a daughter, Hilary, by his first marriage.'

'Where can I find her?' Frank asked. 'And Robin too. Anyone at all who knew my sister.'

'Best to start at Arrowcross Farm, I should think, in the village of Arrowcross,' Mark said. 'Max Blanchard is dead, but his widow, Norah, still lives there so far as I know.'

Gloria asked: 'Would you say, Mr Nolan, that there's any market for a biography of a writer whose books are all out of print?'

'Frankly, no.'

'If I write one,' said Frank, his eagerness to get started making him forget that his host had little time left, 'would you, as an agent, show it to one or two publishers for me?'

'I'm out of the business altogether, Mr Hatfield: have been ever since this miserable cancer caught up with me. Nature forgives us our youthful excesses, but if we continue them into our maturity she eventually sends us the bill. Have you noticed that she always provides a killer disease?'

'We mustn't tire Mr Nolan, darling. He's been very kind to us,' Gloria cautioned.

'Lissern! I'm only too glad to talk about a woman I liked and admired,' Mark stated, with something akin to the gusto that had until recently been characteristic of him. 'I'll tell you all I know, but that isn't much, because Dorothy Blanchard was the most private person ever created. Dilly was a star in the literary firmament. She became the most famous of what I used to call my Family of Writers, and she'd never have lost her lead over the others if she hadn't lost interest in being Mary Orchard.'

'I'll just ask one or two more questions, Mr Nolan, if that's all right with you,' Frank ventured.

'Fire away. Sarah will join us for tea at four o'clock and she'll be able to add a little detail as far as concerns

Arrowcross, because we often spent weekends there when Max Blanchard was alive. We'll ask her what she thinks of your biography idea. Sarah used to be a reader at Sandrew Morath.'

'Then we'll go and look at 38 Willow Square,' Gloria told Frank. 'That'll keep us out of mischief till supper time.'

She had forgotten it would be dark by the time they returned to her car.

4

'Hey! D'you see what I see, Frankie?' she exclaimed, as they drove into Willow Square next morning. 'Number 38 is for sale.'

'So? Are you thinking of buying it?'

'Well, of course we are! Why else would we want to view it? What's that you're writing in your notebook? The agent's name?'

'I'll give him a ring this afternoon.'

'Never mind him, you old silly! Leave it to a consummate liar to do the talking. We're Mr and Mrs Raby this morning in case the owners know Dorothy's maiden name was Hatfield and put two and two together.'

Gloria parked outside number 36 because a red-haired boy of ten or so was kicking and heading a football outside Dorothy's former home and making no attempt to move out of the way.

'You won't damage our nice new car, will you?' Gloria asked, smiling at him.

'A rotten old BMW?' he retorted, challenging her with a stare as cold as it was impudent. 'I'll set fire to it.'

Ball under arm, he followed the couple up the half dozen stone steps leading to a black front door. The house looked well-kept, as did the boy. Through the ground floor windows, Gloria glimpsed silver and polished mahogany.

'Wanna buy it?' the boy demanded, loudly, watching Frank press the bell-push. 'It'll cost you.'

The door was opened by a mature woman, clearly the boy's mother and soon to be a mother again. Her inviting smile suggested that people were not climbing over one another to get at the property.

'They wanna case the joint,' the boy stated, noisily bouncing his ball.

'I've asked you not to play with that outside, Renton,' his mother reminded him. 'You'll have the neighbours complaining again.' Then, to the visitors: 'Did you want to see over the house?'

'I haven't let on about the damp in the cellar or the ghost in the attic,' Renton said.

Using her charm and natural good manners, Gloria followed an apology for calling without an appointment with the explanation that 'my husband and I' had just spotted the property and were leaving London next day.

It worked.

'I'm Eleanor Cross. Please come inside. I'll just close the door.'

'It'll set you back a cool quarter of a million,' Renton warned, having entered with them.

He took three steps along the black-and-white tiled hall before violently kicking the football into the solid wall at the end.

'I wish you wouldn't do that, Renton,' Mrs Cross said, nervously. 'You're marking the paint. I don't know what your father will say if he sees it. Have you any children, Mrs Raby?'

'Three girls,' Gloria answered.

'We'll start here, in the drawing room, on the right.'

Renton preceded them, walking backwards.

'My father drives a Porsche. That can lick a BMW any day,' he said.

It soon became evident that he ran the household. He accompanied the party into every room and was free with his comments, always positioning himself between his mother and the visitors.

'You buy a property as it looks, you know,' he informed them on the stairs. 'If the roof leaks or the lavatory goes through the floor the first time you sit on it, that's your hard luck. I was only kidding about the damp, but not about the ghost.'

'Who lived here before you, Mrs Cross?' Frank asked.

'A couple named Blanchard. Mrs Blanchard wrote stories. My husband tried to find her books in the London Library, but no one there knew anything about her.'

Renton said: 'Her name was Dorothy. Stinking awful name. Her husband did the washing and ironing and lived like a hermit in the basement.'

'That's only what neighbours say,' Mrs Cross cautioned. 'Besides, Mr and Mrs Raby are only interested in the house.'

Her distressed eyes watched her son place his little bottom on a rocking horse that was too small for him and start rocking furiously.

'That's Fiona's and you're going to break it like that,' she lamented. 'I won't tell you again.'

'Are you from the north?' the boy demanded, darting in front of the trio so as to reach the attic ahead of them.

Frank left Gloria to respond.

'Grimepits,' she said. 'An old Yorkshire mining village that is about to be brought up to slum standards.'

Renton pretended to vomit.

'Yorkshire!' he exclaimed, in utmost disgust. 'Grimepits!'

'That's enough, Renton,' his mother warned. 'We can't all live in Tooting Bec or Pratt's Bottom. Here we have the attic.'

Renton barred the doorway with outstretched arms.

'Only German spoken beyond this point,' he declared. 'Unless you want the ghost to appear.'

Mrs Cross told him not to be silly, adding: 'Let Mr and Mrs Raby through, dear.'

'Not without the password,' the boy insisted.

'Wir kennen nicht das Losungswort,' Frank admitted, getting the negative in the wrong place. 'Sie müssen es uns geben.'

Gloria's small, slim hand found its way into his. He had persuaded her to begin learning German with him, her keyboard aspirations having fallen by the wayside.

Renton stepped aside with: 'Kommen Sie bitte herein!'

'The furnishings are exactly as they were when Mrs Blanchard wrote her books here,' his mother explained. 'I operate a translation service, so the layout is just right for me and an assistant. My husband is a Ford executive and is having to spend a lot of time in Germany at the moment.'

Gloria walked to the window on her high heels, her hands in the pockets of her vicuna polo coat, and stood looking out over Willow Square to busy Oratory Road while Frank considered the furniture and started asking questions about the property.

The room was a spacious rectangle, close-fitted with plain grey Wilton. To his right stood two identical mahogany desks, their leather tops matching the green of the steel filing cabinet and tall stationery cupboard. To his left was a sitting area, its salient features being a sofa, a low coffee table and two easy chairs, one to each side of a gas fire.

He was about to remark 'So this is where my sister lived and presumably died', but checked himself and said instead that it was all very businesslike.

'Not to say masculine,' said Mrs Cross. 'Have you seen enough? Mrs Raby – have you?'

Renton wanted to know what Frank did for a living.

'I put the bubbles in spirit levels. Someone has to do it.'

'We bought the house and all her furniture from Mrs Blanchard's executors,' Mrs Cross explained, leading the way back to the hall until, seeing his opportunity on the first landing, her son dodged in front of her. 'We lost every last stick of ours in a dreadful fire. I don't know where your taste in furniture lies, but Jack and I love antiques and so did the Blanchards, as you must have observed. The dining room and drawing room are full of examples.'

'Have we seen everything?' Frank asked, notebook in hand, his index finger slotted between the pages. 'You've told me the asking price and the rates and the house, you say, is freehold.'

Mrs Cross remembered the garage, which was round the back, and the basement.

'Oh, I don't think we need trouble you further,' Gloria told her. 'You've been very kind. We'll be in touch with your agent if we decide to go ahead.'

'No one's allowed in the garage because it's my gang hut, and all there is in the basement is a mouldy old still room where I keep my white mice,' Renton stated, sitting now on his football and surrounded by three pairs of legs.

His fond mother ruffled his hair as Frank and Gloria took their leave.

'Don't you wonder why people have children?' Gloria murmured, slipping her arm through Frank's on the walk back to the BMW. 'I suppose if they didn't they'd be sitting looking at each other. Can you imagine what Dorothy would have done with dear little Renton?'

'Lowered him slowly into a vat of boiling oil. I can appreciate now why certain species eat their young. Mercifully, all children are not like him. Had he lived, my son would've been just about his age today, but Clare and I would never have let him develop like that. I liked the house. Did you?'

'Very Dorothy. Orderly. Cold. Slightly intimidating.'

'What's the betting her husband had to do as he was told?'

'I'm surprised she married, Frank. She was very frightened of men when I knew her.'

Once in the car, the couple sat for a few minutes with the motor running and soft warmth filling the interior.

Gloria lit a cigarette.

'Oh boy, I needed that!' she admitted, after blowing a jet of blue smoke at the open inch of her window. 'Are you still of a mind to write the biography?'

'I don't think so. Not after what Sarah Nolan said about finding a publisher before putting pen to paper. I take her point that most biographies are commissioned from experienced writers. An agreement is drawn up between author and publisher and thereafter they work closely together. It makes sense.'

'You don't fancy knocking on a few publishers' doors before we bid farewell to London, as Mark Nolan suggested? He was rather nice, I thought. Well, they both were.'

Frank was shaking his head. His telephone encounter with Muriel Lint at Marjorie d'Or had not been encouraging.

'I've still got the bruises,' he confessed. 'No. The biography idea is dead and buried.'

Gloria was glad. She had slightly resented Frank's preoccupation with something other than herself. She turned to smile at him and to slip her free hand into his. 'Your hair has been beautifully cut at Trumper's,' she said, content that she had persuaded him to let it grow longer. 'Shall we have lunch at Fortnum's, darling? Later, unless you want to do something else, we could make a few inquiries about a holiday in America.'

Towards the end of the afternoon, before the shops started closing, Frank found himself looking at the new lilac shirts and coordinated ties in Jermyn Street.

Chapter Five

On the Saturday before Christmas, when Frank and Gloria were settling into their suite at Brown's Hotel, Kitty walked out of the Birmingham dry cleaner's for the last time, placed her two bulging shopping bags on the back seat of the Citroën and got in beside Charles Dooley.

She remembered not to kiss his cheek. Although they held hands whenever possible, Dooley didn't approve of kissing outside the home. For a man generally regarded as coarse, there was an unexpected delicacy, even daintiness, about him in certain respects.

'Aren't cars wonderful, Chummy?' Kitty exclaimed, hugging herself. 'All warm and cosy, like little houses on wheels. Is it hard to drive a car? Will you teach me?'

Dooley's silence was her answer. He didn't like women having more mobility than was necessary for looking after their menfolk. Everything had to be to his liking in the home as well as in Kitty's behaviour and aspirations if she were not to incur his displeasure.

'I'll drive through the city centre and let you see the Christmas lights,' he said. 'How d'you feel about starting your nice new job next month? Excited?'

'You bet. More money, more free time, and much more interesting work. Teaching in a catering college'll be just the job and I've got you to thank for spotting the advert and making me write after it. The girls at the cleaner's gave me a little present and a card. I'll show you when we get home, Chummy. What've you done today? – apart from drinking pints of wallop and playing darts at lunch time.'

It had been a normal Saturday. Dooley had spent the morning in the flat, writing his weekly report and falsifying his expenses, and most of the afternoon in the noisy cafeteria at Ketter's Birmingham store, chatting and drinking coffee with the manager. He had bought Christmas presents for Elsie (his former landlady) and Mrs Osborne and yet more clothes for his queen.

'Everything's laid out on the bed,' he told her. 'You'll rub those little hands of yours when you see the frock you're going to wear tonight.'

'Where are we going, Chummy? Oh, just look! Aren't the lights gorgeous!'

'You never seen naffink like this in Gravestone Bay, I know, and you won't see naffink like it in Liverpool neever,' Dooley predicted, lapsing into cockney mispronunciations, as he frequently did when expressing satisfaction, surprise or protest. 'The furver norf you go, the darker it gets, till all they're doin' in Scotland is rubbin' two sticks together.'

'This is High Street. I recognise Marks and Spencer's and Ketter's of course. Where are we going tonight?'

'Now how did I know you'd come back to that question? Where are we going, sweetness? We're going where the pianist plays *Forgotten Dreams* the minute your pretty little face comes round the door. In other words, the Fire Cracker Club.'

'Oh, goody! It's a nice dance floor and I like the jumbo sausages, even if they do put on weight.'

'You'll enjoy tonight's floor show. A special bill to celebrate the anniversary of the opening. Billy Prince. Emmy Reinhardt's Glitter Girls. The Malendreno Twins. Heard o' them, have you?'

'Two handsome men in white tuxedos at white grand pianos. Blond hair, blue eyes with drops in them, and a red carnation in the lapel. Frank took me to see them at the Liverpool Empire on my birthday once.'

'That boring bloke! Cor! What time is it, Kit? I shouldn't wonder if he's in bed by now.'

Kitty bit her lower lip and her eyes were alive with amusement. When she and Charles talked about Frank, it was always to skit at him. Dooley's latest name for him was Mister Better-to-be-safe-than-sorry. He followed this with a guffaw and: 'Who'd be like him? I ask you!'

Kitty hadn't heard of Billy Prince.

'Nah! Billy don't come north unless he has to. He's a song and dance man, Billy, with a line o' rapid patter. Models himself on Max Miller.'

'Emmy Reinhardt's Glitter Girls once stayed at the New Leaf Hotel. At least, the girls did. Emmy had a suite to herself at the Ninian. No glorified boarding houses for Madam, as the girls had to call the old crow.'

'Nice one. Nice one. What's for dinner? I'll stop in a minute and buy the plonk.'

'Aren't you bothered about drinking and driving, Charles?' Kitty ventured, with a squeak of amusement in her voice and mindful of the several pints of Davenport's bitter that Dooley would sink at the Fire Cracker. 'I'm only thinking of you and your job.'

'Well, don't. If you want to think about anything at all, think about new ways of pleasing me. Okay?'

Dooley wouldn't let her see her new clothes until after dinner. Then, while he put on black silk socks and patent leather shoes, black braided trousers and frilly white shirt, a midnight blue dinner jacket with matching velvet bow tie and cummerbund, Kitty found herself changing into a completely new outfit, every item of which, nylons apart, matched her blue eyes. She had intended wearing some of the exquisite pearls and diamonds that Frank had given her, but Dooley had provided lapis lazuli earrings, bracelet and necklace, plus a gold plated lapis lazuli wristwatch to go with sequined court shoes and a pleated chiffon cocktail dress.

'You should've been a fashion designer, if y'ask me,' Kitty told him, after they had agreed that she looked strikingly elegant. 'But never buy me anything green, Chummy, not even underwear. I got Clare to make me a green dress when she was married to Frank, but I only wore it once and that was once too often. I wince now when I think I wore green shoes and a green turban with it. It was one of those whopping great mistakes we make sometimes.'

'All eyes'll be on you tonight, Kit. You'll be the belle of the ball.'

There was dancing before and after the floor show, but the floor was too small for the number of people wanting to use it, so there was little they could do save shuffle their feet. Dooley was no dancer anyway. While his right arm was round Kitty's waist, his left hand was holding her right hand and pumping it up and down. At the same time, he was watching other dancers as well as patrons drinking at the bar or seated at tables arranged round the dance floor.

He kissed her ear and murmured into it: 'Every bird in the place wants to put a dagger between your shoulders and every bloke wants to put his between your thighs.'

'That isn't nice, Chummy,' Kitty said, lowering her eyes.

Dooley the Undaunted replied: 'A soldier calls his prick his mutton dagger.'

'I still don't like it.'

Kitty moved a little closer. She and Dooley were not in love, but each found rest and stimulation in the other's company. Dooley liked providing for a woman whose welcome-home was overt and genuine. He was proud of her looks as well as her personality. As for Kitty herself, her pleasure lay not only in keeping herself silky for him, but equally in feeding his voracious appetite and in making their flat as comfortable as their means and her feminine flair could contrive. Ketter's paid the telephone account, Dooley paid the rent, and Kitty's income was her housekeeping money.

'Am I a good wife?' she asked.

'Wotcha arskin me for? Arsk ya bleedin' azband.'

'You know what I mean, silly.'

Dooley looked down at her, sniffed, and curled his upper lip.

'You're not bad, I s'pose,' he sneered.

Then his large pink face with its very white false teeth broke into a smile as he gave her a squeeze and said: 'You'll do till samfink better comes along.'

Although unfailingly pleasant, he seldom laughed. The closest he normally came to laughter was the chuckle that Kitty heard now. It was a sizzling sound made in the sides of the mouth and she liked it. He never asked Kitty if she was satisfied with him because it never occurred to him to ask himself.

'When d'you start at the catering college?' he asked.

'Sixth of January. What they call a new term.'

'I go back to work on the second with the annual survey at our Kendal store. It'll be an all-day job. We'll make an early start and stay overnight at the Beech Hill Hotel.'

Delighted, Kitty squeaked: 'You mean you'll take me with you?'

'If you're a good girl. You'll like the Beech Hill. They have log fires at this time of the year and a lovely view over Lake Windermere.'

'Oh, I've got so much to look forward to! My new job, Christmas with Mum in Liverpool, and my first look at the Lake District.'

But more immediately there was the next day. Kitty loved Sunday more than any other day of the week. She and Charles rose late. After breakfast she ironed Friday night's washing while Dooley took the Cit to the car wash and filled the tank with petrol. Then they set off for a traditional roast luncheon at one of the numerous hostelries known to Charles in and around Birmingham, sometimes venturing as far as Warwick or Shrewsbury, the destination always being kept secret from Kitty.

'I'm eating and drinking too much,' she admitted, when they were back at their table and about to enjoy the keyboard wizardry of the Malendreno Twins. 'I'm getting fat, Chummy.'

But not, she reflected, with child. The couple made love on Friday and Sunday nights and Dooley was riding bareback, as he put it, meaning without contraception. He was a roll-on roll-off partner, unadventurous and caring only for his own pleasurable relief, but Kitty responded vigorously, digging her nails into the soft white flesh of his back, biting, and using her bare heels to kick him forward and upward, ever hopeful that she would presently conceive.

Had she? As midnight passed and the Malendreno Twins rose as one to acknowledge gathering applause, she crossed her fingers and mentally ticked off another day.

2

'Where is he?' Mrs Osborne began, the grim determination of her tone suggesting she had decided overnight to murder him.

She was entering her cheerless living room to start another day of brooding and complaining at the fireside.

'Charles has had to go to London again,' Kitty answered.

'What's going on down there? It's the second time this week.'

'Business, I suppose. He said he'd be back about five. Can I get you anything, Mum? I'll make the coffee at eleven.'

She was working on her knees in front of the fire, raking out brown and grey ash before adding fresh coals and sweeping the tiled hearth.

'When I opened the curtains and saw his car gone from outside, I thought he'd left you,' her mother said, contentedly.

She wound the clock that stood on her mantelpiece, flanked now on both sides by Christmas cards. One of them, addressed only to her, was from Frank Hatfield. Then she lowered herself into her broken-down armchair – a high-backed curiosity of raw wood and faintly ecclesiastical appearance, the frayed webbing of its seat overlaid with old newspapers and flattened cushions – and gazed mournfully at the fire. A cold creature even in summer, Connie Osborne, aged sixty, with dull eyes and black hair shot with grey, wore a shawl round her jumper and cardigan, a winter skirt, stockings wrinkled at the knees and soft slippers lined with imitation fur.

'Try to make Charles welcome, Mother. He's got feelings the same as anyone else. We're only here for a few days and he's very nice to you,' Kitty said. 'That was a lovely Christmas present he brought you from Birmingham and it must've cost a packet of money.'

'He's your choice. That doesn't mean I have to like him, present or no present. He's a London know-all. A barrow boy. I've taken my rent book up to my room, where it'll stay till he leaves my house.'

'Oh, for heaven's sake, Mother! Charles only glanced at it as we were putting our coats on to go out,' Kitty protested, standing up, dustpan and hearth brush in hand. 'What's so terrible about that?'

'He had no rights looking at it, let alone picking it up and seeing inside. What I pay for this house is my concern and no one else's.'

Prior to the outrage, its resting place had been beside the milk money on top of the glove drawer beneath the centrally mounted mirror of the big, old-fashioned hallstand. 'Just checkin' to see you're not bein' done, Connie,' Dooley had explained, having turned to find Mrs Osborne glaring at him as he closed and replaced the book. 'No flesh broken, sweetness. No offence meant and none taken, I'm sure.'

Mrs Osborne hated his familiarity, his unusual expressions, and especially his cockney whine and intonation. 'London folks are not like us,' she once observed; and here was living proof of that judgement.

'We'll see you later, Mum,' Kitty had said, in the act of pulling the front door closed. 'I want Charles to see Chantry's.'

The couple set off in cold, hard sunshine, hand in hand and with Mrs Osborne's elderly dog, Roddy, on a lead. Five minutes later, they were standing with their backs to a public house called The Brown Penny and looking across busy Waverton Road at what had once been Chantry's Dancing School. The stone building, standing four-square in a walled garden, had recently reverted to a private residence and its original name, Chantry House, had been restored.

'I taught at the school in the evenings after work,' Kitty said, omitting to mention that she had done so without pay. 'My somebody-special ran it – Clive Rolls. We were going to get married when he died. See those windows up on the roof, Chummy? That's where Clive lived. In the attic flat.'

She waited for Dooley to ask if she still thought of Clive, but, a little to her dismay, he didn't. Had he done so, she would have replied that Clive seldom entered her thoughts these days and she hadn't looked at his photograph since leaving the New Leaf Hotel. Indeed, she wasn't sure if she'd brought it with her.

'And it was here you met Frank Nobody, Esquire,' Dooley

declared, loudly and joyfully. 'Tell me, pretty maiden: did he come to you to be taught the minuet or was it the yearning saunter? Cor!'

Kitty squeezed Charles's hand and told him he was awful, but this time she didn't join him in his scoffing. The sight of Chantry's had stirred her conscience. Frank, already engaged to Clare Mason, had fallen completely and helplessly in love with Kitty, had never lived through emotional turbulence like it and never would again. Throughout their clandestine affair, she had teased him pitilessly, openly skitting at his seriousness and delighting in making him wait for dates. She comforted herself now with the reminder that she had never said she loved him, even after they were married and trying for a baby. As she and Charles continued their walk, she wondered if Frank had got her out of his system as she had got Clive Rolls out of hers.

Convinced that her daughter secretly regretted leaving Frank, Mrs Osborne used Dooley's absence in London to make another attempt at getting Kitty to return to him.

'Ring him up now. Or let me,' she urged. 'He'll have you back, Cath, of course he will.'

'But I don't want to go back. How many times must I tell you, Mother? Frank's too tame. I could've done as I liked with Frank if I'd been that sort of woman. I like a masterful man.'

'You mean a man who expects you to dance attendance on him? You mean a man who gets into his car and drives off without a word of explanation? Is that what you mean?'

'It's my life, Mother. Here's your coffee.'

'Well, I'm glad it's not mine, that's all. Give me Frank Hatfield any day.'

Connie had spent a fortnight every summer at the New Leaf Hotel without ever finding anything to criticise in the son-in-law who called her Mum and wouldn't even let her pay for drinks from the bar.

'The way he used to help you . . .' she told the fire, shaking her head. 'How many times have I heard him say "I'll do that, Cath. You go and sit down"? I could see this one saying it. He'll have you washing his car and cleaning his shoes before you're much older, mark my words.'

'Charles doesn't get it all his own way,' said Kitty, who, partly by pretending that she didn't like his living in the same city as Mary Singleton, was slowly persuading him to buy a house in Liverpool. 'He only thinks he does.'

She was discovering areas in which he was dependent upon her, one of them being the letter-writing that had suddenly become necessary. They had both left school at fourteen, but Kitty's English had steadily improved thanks to five years of listening to Frank's correct use of tenses and past participles. To his embarrassment, Dooley still wrote in capitals, never having mastered longhand. While careful not to let her see the text of his letters, he had been asking lately for Kitty's help with spelling and grammar and had merrily christened her Dooley's Dictionary of Difficult Words.

He enjoyed television, finding speech easier to follow than print and, like Kitty, recognising its value in promoting fluency and enlarging the vocabulary. Sitting holding hands, they watched *Z Cars*, *All Gas & Gaiters* and *News at Ten*, while Connie pointedly read the *Liverpool Echo*. When alone, she rarely switched on 'that damned thing', preferring her library book and claiming that television, because it provided the word as well as the image, put the imagination to sleep. Even sound radio was less harmful, since it left the listener to picture the scene. Literature, she maintained, was the only medium to fully engage the imagination, the printed page being the umbilical cord between reader and writer.

'You'll never know anything unless you read,' she said.

Kitty looked sidelong at her man, expecting this mention of books to bring out the worst in him. But then she remembered the oriental respect he had for the older generation and was not surprised to hear him respond with tolerance and even generosity. 'Tell you what, Connie my love: we'll buy you a big-screen colour telly and watch your opinion change. She'll become a regular telly-girl, won't she, Kit?'

'I'm perfectly content with what I have, thank you,' Mrs Osborne replied, coldly.

'Oh, come off it, sweetness! A twelve-inch screen? Black and white? Cor, the thing's a museum piece.'

Mrs Osborne, after glaring at Dooley's profile for a minute or more, began gathering herself together for bed.

'I'll go up now, Cath, and see you in the morning,' she said, making steadily for the door.

As always, she retired with a glass of water and a folded sheet of newspaper from the supply beneath the cushions of her chair. The water was to ease the bouts of heavy coughing that regularly disturbed her sleep. When Dooley discovered the purpose of the newspaper, he further alienated her by chirping: 'We shall have to buy you a spittoon, Connie, as well as a noo telly.'

Kitty followed her to the door, asking her quietly to say goodnight to Charles, who duly acknowledged her blunt and grudging compliance with: 'Mind how you go, love. Sleep well and God bless, eh?'

When they were alone, he told Kitty that the place needed more than a new television. 'Where did her furniture come from? Out o' the bleed'n Ark, I shouldn't wonder. Might have been made from the original timber.'

'It's all forty years old.'

'What? And the rest. I reckon it was second hand when it was noo. And what about the pets? Place is more like Whipsnade.'

'Roddy and the cat were strays.'

'Roddy stinks.'

'I know. But Mum's grown old with him and doesn't notice.'

'She's old before her time, Kit. How long's she been sittin' in that sawn-off sentrybox over there? That belongs in the Guinness Book of Records. If she breaks wind hard enough, she'll fall clean through it.'

'Mum's been at home for three or four years – ever since her cough got worse and she had to give up the flower shop she had in Exchange Station. She'd be doing herself a favour if she'd get out more, instead of just toddling round to the shops.'

'She'd be doing herself a favour if she'd open the winders. Where's your farver?'

'Dead. He was an engineer on Wallasey Ferries.'

'He had blue eyes and black curly hair and a turned-up nose.'

'Yes to the eyes and hair, no to the nose. I got that from my Auntie Flo, Mum's sister, who had the New Leaf Hotel before Frank bought it.'

'That boring bloke! Must we talk about him? Where's Flo now?'

'Retired and living in Wales. What about you, Chummy? You never mention your family. Don't you ever go and see your father in London?'

Dooley looked at his watch and said: 'Time we was climbing the little wooden hill.'

'Ah, that's not fair! You're like a doctor or a detective. You ask questions but don't answer them.'

'Why bovver arskin' 'em then? Come on!'

3

The couple were back at Connie's towards the end of June, by which time Kitty was six months pregnant and they were looking for a house. Although Liverpool was not as central as Birmingham for Dooley's coverage of his territory, Ketter's were sympathetic to Kitty's desire to be near her mother when the baby came, and Dooley himself had no preference outside 'dear ole L-a-a-ndon.' 'If I'm stuck wiv livin' in the norf, it don't matter a toss wevver it's Liverpool, Leeds or Manchester. They're just as boring as each other.'

'A fine bed you've made for yourself, my girl!' Mrs Osborne exclaimed, while she and Kitty were walking home laden with the weekend meat and groceries. 'A baby on the way and you're not even married! He could walk out on you tomorrow and you'd have no claim on him whatsoever.'

'Charles would hardly buy a house, Mother, if he intended walking out on me. I don't know what you've got against him all the time. He likes you. He says you're a character. And he's always pleasant with you. You might at least answer him when he speaks to you, instead of closing your eyes and turning your head away.'

'He got you away from the finest husband a woman could wish for. And what proof have you got that he's going to buy a house? That's only what he tells you and you know what you're like. If he said the Earth was flat, you'd believe him. D'you want my honest opinion, Cath?'

'I think I'm going to get it anyway.'

'I think he's brought you here to leave you here. It wouldn't surprise me one iota if you woke up one morning and found him gone. Why was he up and down to his precious London – twice! – when the both of you were here at Christmas? Why was he writing letters? – a man who can hardly spell his own name. Well, if he does leave you, at least you'll be here with me.'

'His father died,' Kitty explained, patiently. 'He left Charles his house in a place called Harrow-on-the-Hill and Charles has sold it.'

'Did he tell you this himself? I'll bet he didn't. That's another thing I dislike about the man. He comes and goes as he pleases, he tells you nothing and you stand for it.'

'If you must know, I steamed open one of his letters. You might also like to know, Mother, that Charles has already bought a house. I'll know where it is when he comes home tonight.'

Flabbergasted, Mrs Osborne stopped dead to stare in disbelief at her daughter.

'Are you telling me, Catherine, that he's bought a house you haven't even seen?' she demanded.

'Charles says I'll know it when I see it, so it must be one of the ones we've been to see at weekends.'

'Well, I've never heard of behaviour like this in all my life! What if you don't like it when you see it?'

'I have every confidence in Charles, Mother.'

'I can hardly believe my ears. You mean to say you're prepared to live in a house you haven't seen? You'll soon have a baby to consider. Have you thought of that? And where is this house? It could be in Coxside. How d'you know it isn't damp or alive with vermin? Really, Cath, you take some understanding!'

'Charles will explain everything this evening, Mother. He's a Clerk of Works, remember. He'll know what he's buying. Let's walk on.'

'A Clerk of Works is a failed bricklayer,' Mrs Osborne

snapped, having consulted the retired hod carrier who lived three doors up. 'He's nothing'

Once again, she stopped abruptly – this time as she and Kitty turned the corner from Waverton Road into Burnett Road. A short and a long ladder were resting against the facade of number 4 and painters were engaged in scraping and burning off the existing paint.

The startled women bore down on them. Her face tight with anger and consternation, Mrs Osborne demanded to know what the men thought they were doing.

'This is my house. Who sent you here?'

'Father Christmas,' answered the man on the short ladder.

'We don't know, love,' the older man called down. 'We just go where we're sent.'

'Too right,' sneered short ladder. 'We could be paint'n Niagara Falls this time tamorrer.'

'The rent collector said nothing to me about painting,' Mrs Osborne protested. 'All six houses were painted not six months ago. Are you doing the rest of them?'

'Just yours, love.'

'I'm going to talk to Mr Last at Northern Estates,' Connie said to her daughter.

She hurried upstairs to fetch her rent book, then came down to dial the telephone number printed on its front cover.

'Engaged! You might know,' she snapped at Kitty, and slammed the receiver down.

She went outside to ask the older man what colour the house was to be painted. Having had enough of her, he left his mate to reply.

'Red and cream. Told yer it was Daddy Crimbo sent us.'

'Take no notice of him,' Kitty said, as her mother charged back into the house. 'He thinks he's clever.'

'This is a mistake,' Connie decided, dialling again. 'They've got the wrong house or the wrong road.'

Mr Last came on the line. He said he knew nothing about the matter.

'But you're the landlord's agent. Speak to Mr Smush and find out what's going on or give me his number and I'll speak to him. I can't have my home looking like a post office.'

'Mr Smush isn't your landlord any more, Mrs Osborne, and we're not acting for the new owner. Just a moment. I have the property file on my desk. Somewhere. Here. His telephone number is Waverton 1714.'

'But that's my number! It's the number I'm calling from.'

'And his name is Charles Dooley.'

Chapter Six

Their morning appointment at Hamilton Jupp Incorporated, of Massingham Avenue, Manhattan, was with a marketing executive who styled himself Neen Savage the Fourth and who kept them waiting for several minutes in a spacious and tastefully furnished reception area rather resembling that of the nearby hotel in which they would shortly spend their last night in the United States.

Restless as always, Gloria asked if she might smoke.

'Smoking is not permitted anywhere in the building. The same goes for the restrooms. Okay?' the receptionist answered, in a hostile voice that brooked no argument.

Her name, according to a plaque on her expensive desk, was Fragrance Zitroni. She was about as feminine as a jock strap and so vast that it was impossible to tell where flesh left off and her billowing, floor-length dress took over. Her breasts were drooping cones resting on her inflated stomach. Frank would later remark that she was the latest example of what he and Gloria had christened The Balloon People of America. In four weeks of sightseeing by train, Greyhound bus and hired car, they had seen so many grossly fat men and women as to lose count, the most advanced among them being so huge as to be scarcely able to walk.

'Fragrance makes Mavis de Lapp look like Twiggy,' Frank commented, shielding his mouth with his hand. 'How is Mavis, by the way?'

She had telephoned Gloria the night before from Osprey Court, where she had her elderly parents for company.

Although they lived in Redstone Bay, Gloria felt they would enjoy a change of scene and especially the breath-catching views across the Irish Sea to the sunset. The old lady was failing and Mavis herself wasn't too well.

'She suffers with her breathing, you know. All that blubber she carts around . . .' Gloria said, looking round approvingly at the art glass windows, the several attractive pictures and the oiled teak furniture that stood on a wall-to-wall carpet with a Greek key pattern in tan on a yellow ground. 'New York publishers do themselves rather well, nicht wahr? I'm dying to see what Neen Savage the Fourth is like.'

Frank murmured: 'I suspect this is the gent now.'

It was.

'Gloria and Frank? Neen Savage. Sorry you had to wait,' he began, combing his close-cropped ginger hair as he approached. 'I've ordered coffee and it'll be right along. Now suppose you tell me what I can do for you and, more important, what you can do for Hamilton Jupp Incorporated.'

Neen was of average height and bulk, with an Irish-American face: clean-cut features, freckles, tombstone teeth and a button nose that was too small for its surroundings. He would be thirty next birthday. Throughout the interview, he wore sunglasses and a reassuring smile. His light grey worsted suit was unusual for the period, comprising narrow trousers with turn-ups and a single-breasted jacket fastened with four black buttons but without a collar and lapels. He wore a black turtleneck sweater in place of a shirt. A printed card pinned to the jacket thanked you for not smoking. Otherwise, Gloria liked him.

He sat down facing his visitors, who were settled in a low two-seater sofa with brown velvet upholstery that complemented Gloria's blond hair, ivory skin and trim two-piece in fawn linen.

Frank said: 'As I mentioned over the telephone, Mr Savage—'

'Neen.'

'Neen. I'm Mary Orchard's brother and my thoughts about writing her biography have been revived by the success her novels are having on this side of the Atlantic.'

Savage's smile became smug.

'The huge success, Frank,' he contentedly corrected. 'And let's not kid ourselves: it's a fad, a craze; and as such, my friends, it'll quickly burn itself out. Meanwhile, we at Hamilton Jupp are busily stoking the fire.'

'We saw stacks of her novels everywhere we went in America – even in hotel gift shops, even at supermarket check-outs,' Gloria said. 'At home, Mary Orchard is completely forgotten, and you seem to be saying she'll meet the same fate over here within a very short time.'

She was flirting outrageously with Savage, flashing her blue eyes at him and teasing him with her legs, admirably displayed thanks to a skirt so mini that Frank said it was little more than a pelmet. Neen had difficulty in looking at anything else and was relieved when the arrival of coffee provided a temporary distraction.

Gloria offered to pour and pass while Neen explained that the enthusiasm for Mary Orchard's schoolgirl fiction had been sparked by the showing of a television film, made in England in the 1960s, of *Fun & Games at Walker's Croft*.

'Will you believe me when I tell you there are Mary Orchard clubs in girls' high schools, Mary Orchard tee shirts, Mary Orchard straw hats?' he went on, incredulously. 'An all-about-Mary-Orchard biography would hit the rafters, but only if it's on sale within weeks of this moment. How soon can you let me have a first draft, Frank?'

Between sips of excellent coffee, Gloria had started biting her nails. Testily now, she reminded Frank that he knew nothing whatever about writing a biography.

'I can give it my best shot, Gloria. God loves a trier. I still have the notes I made in London.'

'Pity,' Gloria muttered.

'Let me first define biography,' Neen said. 'There is the deep biographical study that tells the reader as much about the protagonist as about his contemporaries and the times he lived in and can take two, maybe three, years to write. That's not what we're talking about right now. What Hamilton Jupp would be interested in publishing is a life-story-with-pictures, printed on art paper in coffee table format. It's got to be racy, romantic, exciting. What's called in the trade a hit-and-run-job.'

'You can't do that,' Gloria told Frank. 'You're too staid.'

'He doesn't have to, Gloria. All I want from Frank is the raw material. We'll write the book in-house. But your name'll be on the cover, Frank, and you'll get the cash. More coffee?'

'Your coffee and your orange juice: those are the things I like best about American catering, Mr Savage,' said Gloria, refilling their cups. Then, echoing his question: 'What have we seen? What haven't we? Everything short of Death Row and the Petrified Forest. Frank likes to visit the homes of novelists, so we've toured Malabar Farm in Ohio and Beauregard House in New Orleans, where Frances Parkinson Keyes wrote *Steamboat Gothic*. She pronounced Keyes to rhyme with eyes, which is an achievement in itself.'

'We love the States. Our first visit, but it won't be our last,' Frank said. 'Tonight, after dark, we're going up to the top of the Empire State Building to see the whole of Manhattan lit up. We've been told it's one of the sights of the world.'

Neen's smile turned sheepish. He said: 'I must confess I've never seen it.'

'We lived for years in Liverpool without ever seeing the Grand National, yet people come from all over the world to see that one race,' Frank remarked.

Savage asked him if his sister had ever visited the United States.

'Dorothy never went anywhere,' Gloria muttered, sulkily.

'These are things I'll have to find out, Neen,' Frank replied. 'We sail for Liverpool on the Emerald Seas tomorrow. Gloria knew my sister well, so we'll pool our memories on the voyage and get on her trail again as soon as we're back in the UK. D'you think I'll need anyone's permission to write the book?'

'I doubt it, Frank, but I'll speak with our legal department and cable you yes or no aboard the Emerald Seas.'

Neen stood up and shook hands.

'Shall I have Fragrance call you a cab?'

'That would be very welcome,' Gloria said. 'And I'm dying for a fag.'

The couple rode down in the lift and positioned themselves just inside the clear glass entrance doors, aware of the stone-cracking heat outside and glad of air conditioning.

'What a flirt you are!' Frank scolded, playfully, sensing that Gloria wanted his attention.

'I didn't do anything,' she protested.

She took Frank's hand and he smiled down at her.

'You don't have to,' he said, tenderly. 'Nature did it for you.'

'I'm not bad for my age.'

'You're remarkable. Poor Neen Savage the Fourth! I'll bet he's standing under a cold shower at this very moment.'

'I attribute my eternal youth to sex, alcohol and no exercise. My fear, Frankie darling, is that I may prove to be a female Dorian Gray.'

'I'm going back to that bookshop, Gloria, and buy a copy of each of Dorothy's books.'

'Have a lovely time. I'm going back to our suite and a Gordon's gin with crushed ice and lemon.'

'Here's our taxi.'

'Thank God! A cigarette at last!'

She had one between her lips and was about to click the silver lighter Frank had given her for her birthday when he pointed out a notice fixed to the driver's partition thanking passengers for not smoking.

2

Their stateroom aboard Emerald Seas comprised a bedroom with a king size bed, a day room big enough to walk about in, and a combined bathroom and lavatory. Frank rose at eight, jogged round the promenade deck for ten minutes, then showered, shaved and dressed before eating a cooked breakfast with mango juice and black coffee at the table. Unlike Gloria, he could never bring himself to eat in bed. For a reason he was unable to identify, it struck him as unclean.

He had settled to his writing at the cleared table when eventually Gloria emerged from the bedroom, still in her frilly black nightdress. All warm and soft, she closed in behind him, put her arms over his shoulders and kissed his ear.

'And when squire came home from the chase, he pleasured me twice in his jackboots,' she said, softly.

Frank concealed his annoyance behind a smile and tried to continue with his work.

'You like saying that, don't you?' he asked, from a distance.

'The scene is the farmhouse kitchen and he's got me over the table.'

'Where did you get it from?'

'Oh, I forget. *The Church Times*, I think. What does it matter?'

'There's some coffee left, Glorious.'

'Don't want coffee.'

What she did want became explicit when the kissing spread to his cheek and her porky little hands invaded his trousers.

'Not again, love!' Frank protested, gently disengaging himself from her coils. 'You've got me worn out. I don't know how Raby kept up with you, unless he had hollow legs filled with love juice, as you call it.'

'Ah, Frankie! Frankie, darling . . .'

Gloria was crooning endearments and brushing the side of Frank's face with her hair as her arms made another attempt at ensnaring him.

'Look! It's all right for you,' he snapped, again releasing himself. 'You just lie there while I bounce around.'

'I do not just lie there and you know it. I'll bet I put more into it than your two wives rolled together,' Gloria retorted, raising her voice. 'You didn't know what love-making was till you got into bed with me. Well, you're not the only man on the ship. Put that in your notebook.'

She poured herself some coffee, lit a cigarette and plumped down in one of the easy chairs that matched a sofa upholstered in cream suede with black contour piping.

Frank went on writing. A minute or more passed in silence while Gloria watched him steadily and without love. Then:

'What was Cath like?' she asked, sharply. 'I gather she was rather common.'

Frank hesitated, as she knew he would.

'What makes you think that, Gloria?' he asked, quietly.

'The man she cleared off with. You've called him a brute, among other things. I'm trying to account for the attraction. She didn't care for you, did she?'

'Evidently not.'

'D'you want to know why it's obvious?'

'I'm waiting.'

'She let you dress like a private soldier. The prison haircut. The spit-and-polish shoes. They were a dead give-away.'

'Really? If that's true, I have you to thank for raising me from the ranks.'

'Don't think it has any significance. I got you out of starched white shirts and elastic armbands simply because I didn't want to be seen with a shop assistant on his afternoon off. You mean nothing more to me than the ship's masseur.'

'Did you enjoy your session with him yesterday? What's his name, by the way? Nut Smorgasbord or Snor Maelstrom? Oh, I forgot! A lady doesn't ask questions with her mouth full.'

Gloria tensed like a threatened spider.

'One more crack like that and I walk straight through that door,' she breathed.

'Open it first, Gloria.'

There was a knock on it.

'Who d'you suppose this is?' Frank murmured, getting up from the table.

'Find out. And the word is whom.'

It was their steward with a cable from Neen Savage the Fourth.

NO LEGAL OBSTACLE TO AUTHORING LIFE STORY ALL RIGHTS BOUGHT BY HAMILTON JUPP FROM MRS IDA PRINCE ONE YEAR PAST GET BUSY KEEP IN TOUCH REGARDS SAVAGE.

Frank was smiling at the text as Gloria, her anger simmering behind a tight face, brushed past him on her way to the bedroom.

'Interesting, isn't it,' he said, 'that Dorothy left the rights to her secretary rather than her husband?'

Gloria paused in the threshold and turned to look coldly at him.

'I'm sure it changes the course of history. Incidentally,' she added, 'you don't open the door to a steward. You call to him to come in.'

'But suppose it isn't the steward?'

'Who else can it be? You *were* a shop assistant, weren't you?'

She might have been accusing him of a felony. Without giving him time to answer, she announced that she was going to dress, continuing with: 'If you fancy a shipboard romance with one of the scullery maids, feel free to carry on. You can bring her here. I'll willingly sit in the bar for as long as it takes.'

She slammed the door.

Frank put aside his writing when presently she came back into the day room. Standing up, he told her she looked nice, adding that Cath couldn't wear green.

'I'm too old for pink and too depraved for white,' she remarked, fastening an amber-on-gold-plate bracelet while walking towards Frank on high heels. Along with a matching necklace and eight colourful knuckledusters, it represented the day's selection of costume jewellery. In the evening, when she and Frank dressed for dinner, Gloria would wear the brilliants that spent most of the voyage locked in the wardrobe safe.

'Come on!' she said, back to her old happy-sad self. 'My tummy's starting to eat itself.'

'M'lady should eat breakfast. Most important meal of the day. It breaks a fast of twelve, even fourteen, hours: hence its name.'

'Aren't you clever? You've a well-stocked mind, dear, and an informing voice. Did Cath ever tell you you're a pain in the neck?'

'Every hour on the hour. She was good like that.'

'For luncheon, I'm going to order black pudding with a dollop of tomato sauce on top and watch their faces.'

Gloria slipped her arm through Frank's as they made their way to the bar and out onto the sundeck.

'D'you still think about Cath?' she asked, lighting one of her Fribourg & Treyer cigarettes. Knowing American tobacco to be too strong for her taste, she had packed a month's supply of her favourite Number One Filter de Luxe in her splendid Louis Vuitton luggage. 'Would you go back to the old life? Tell me true, Frankie dear.'

They sat down and the iced champagne cocktails arrived.

Frank said: 'I'm an honest man and I accept what you said about me before. I don't agree that Cath is common, but there's no denying she seems ordinary compared to you. No, Gloria, I wouldn't go back. Cheers!'

3

After a fortnight at Osprey Court, the couple headed south on Frank's renewed quest for biographical material. Mindful of Savage's cable, he would have liked to have started sooner, but Gloria needed a breathing space and he was aware that she tolerated rather than shared his enthusiasm for interviews with Ida Prince, Robin Blanchard and Robin's stepmother, Norah Blanchard, who was first on Frank's list.

'Mark Nolan was very helpful,' he said, when they were motoring past Cannock on the M6.

'You decided to telephone him then? I know you were worried about disturbing him,' Gloria answered. 'Mind you, in his condition, poor man, he's probably glad of any diversion.'

'I spoke with him this morning while you were down in the garage with Mavis, emptying the Humber Estate. Are you going to let her use the BMW in future?'

'Why not? I like her to take her parents for drives and the BMW will be easier for them to get in and out of. More comfortable too.'

'What d'you think of your smart new Morgan so far? Is it up to expectations?'

Gloria was frowning.

'I'm watching this simpleton in front,' she explained. 'I reckon to meet one certifiable idiot a day and at least three runners-up. The Morgan? Superb. You should learn to drive, darling. It's fun, especially in an open car and in weather like this. I came across my first licence the other day, Frank – the one I got after passing my test in April 1951. It's quite amusing. Filled in in ink and gummed into a little red book with the City of Liverpool crest on the cover. I passed in Group A, so I'm entitled to drive a heavy locomotive, light locomotive, heavy motor car, light motor car, motor tractor and a motor tricycle with means of reversing. They forgot the steam roller.'

'There's a police car behind.'

'How unromantic you are!'

They had collected the Morgan Plus Eight earlier in the day from Ralph Cannan's motor showrooms in Liverpool. Mavis had tailed them from Redstone Bay in the Humber, parting with it to Nigel Cannan before driving the BMW back to Osprey Court. 'Watch her drinking, Frank, won't you?' she had murmured, while Nigel was handing over the new car to Gloria. 'It's taking off again.'

'Did you manage to get us a hotel, Frankie?' Gloria remembered to ask when they were south of Birmingham.

'Mark mentioned the Station Hotel at Wall Town, which is only a short drive from Arrowcross Farm, and that's where Norah Blanchard lives. God willing, she'll lead us to Robin and Ida.'

'But did you get us a room, dear?'

'Oh, yes. I thought two nights would do till we see what develops. You want to move on anyway, don't you, to see Jamaica Inn? I'll ring Norah as soon as we reach the hotel. Mark thinks she'll see me all right when I say I'm Robin's brother-in-law.'

In Redstone Bay, Frank had continued the loose writing begun aboard Emerald Seas, blending his memories of Dorothy with those of Gloria. He had worked in her dining room, where the pale English oak furniture, all of it custom made for the family home in Mayfields, stood on a Nain carpet, hand woven in silk and wool on cotton, its medallion design employing beige, blue and ivory within a wide border filled with scrolls and curling leaves. The carpet was surrounded by a broad margin of Iroko strip, the table by six side chairs upholstered in yellow Lucchese silk with a wreath of fruit and flowers hand painted on the backs. There was a sideboard, a copper-encased gas fire similar to the one in the drawing room, a ceiling light with matching sconces, and a tall cabinet with a clock inset at the top and a cellaret behind panelled doors at the bottom. In between were glass doors protecting crystal and china on shelves that had borne the family silver until Peter Raby made off with it. He had dismissed as 'antwacky' the pier glass in an embossed silver frame that hung now between the two windows, unaware that it was worth more than the rest of his loot put together.

'He's due out shortly,' Gloria said, when they were back on the motorway following a late luncheon at Michael Wood services. 'I wonder if he'll come looking for me.'

'I'll be there if he does and you know how frightening I can be. When roused, I've been known to rip a newspaper down the middle with my bare hands.'

'Raby's not the sort to resort to fisticuffs. He's a low grade lounge lizard with a taste for made-to-measure shoes and fancy waistcoats. I'm not frightened of him, only of being pestered by him. He'll need money. Is it a problem that I'm still his wife? Has he any claim, marital or otherwise on me or my property? I'll talk to my solicitor, Frank, when we get home.'

'I shouldn't worry, Glorious. He won't get past the guard-room if you tell the concierge you don't want to see him.'

'If he gets that close to me, Frank, he means business, and no amount of security guards will thwart him. I don't call him a gangster for nothing. Raby knows a lot of people, most of them pretty ugly.'

'Why did you marry him?'

'Because I wanted a man, same as every other woman. Don't believe one who says she doesn't.'

'What about lesbians?'

'I know nothing about them. All I know is I like men, all men, sods though they are. I wish there were more men so's I could like them too. Something else you may have noticed – I can't stand being alone. A lot of marriages are held together by the dread of loneliness and by precious little else, in my opinion.'

Before he had made the discovery himself, Mavis de Lapp had warned Frank that Gloria was still a child. Company, novelty and variety were essential if she wasn't to slump into boredom and start looking round for something stronger than coffee.

She was a late riser, sleeping curled up like a cat, so Frank had done his writing before she was ready to go shopping, to swim at the Ninian or just sit smoking and talking till it came time to have luncheon in the residents' rooftop dining room. Sometimes they lunched with Mavis in the apartment, having a light meal sent down from the kitchens or preparing it themselves. True to the pattern set by his first wife, Frank ate a balanced diet whereas Gloria picked at her food, getting through the day mainly on coffee and cigarettes. She claimed that once a month she had a fall of soot. In the evenings, after dinner, they would watch television or play gin rummy until Gloria announced that it was time for 'a little dinky' at nine o'clock or thereabouts. They seldom went out. Once in a while, the two old sticks from downstairs came up for a game of bridge, Mavis making four while Frank read by the fire or out on the balcony.

Weather permitting, the trio played golf on the sand-swept links, taking lessons from the pro, whose name was Billy Bee and on whom Mavis had a hidden crush. Large of frame and red of face, invariably with a cork-tipped cigarette smouldering between his lips, Billy was married with a son in the Parachute Regiment. He sported brogues, Argyle socks with green tabs showing at the tops, brown check plus fours (Frank called them shit catchers) and a cloth cap of similar design and coloration. So as to be near him, Mavis was painting a water colour of the club house from the porch of his golf shop.

'Nigel Cannan's more in my line,' Gloria admitted, when the conversation turned again to the indigo blue Morgan in which she and Frank were now approaching Marlborough. 'I seduced Nigel when he was still at Eton and I was single and living at home. This was before my parents were killed and while I was sleeping with Raby odd afternoons in a cheap hotel in Mount Pleasant. My father and Nigel's father, Ralph Cannan, were chums. Nigel came to Ailsa, our house in Mayfields, one Saturday to collect Daddy's Bentley to take it in for repairs or something and we had a jolly hour together in front of the drawing room fire. He asked me this morning if I remembered it.'

'You're making this up, aren't you?'

A satisfied smile appeared on Gloria's face.

'Cad!' she exclaimed, archly. 'How did you guess?'

'It's a typical Gloria confection. Ralph Cannan, if I'm not mistaken, was one of only three people in Britain to own a Dusenberg.'

'He once gave me a ride in it. Ralph owns half a dozen rare cars, including a Royce and a Reo staff car from the First World War.'

'The Royce must be worth more than Cleopatra's girdle, because only four were made. Ralph Cannan was a governor of the school I went to,' Frank recalled. 'My dad claimed I only got in thanks to their friendship.'

'Which school was this?'

'Mariner's College, Liverpool. Heard of it?'

'Only just.'

'Where did you go? Swandella?'

'Rose Choir. Heard of it?'

'Who hasn't? It's the top boarding school for girls in the country, isn't it? Swandella was always Dorothy's dream and she very nearly got there too. I thought it was one of the best schools around.'

'Around where? It's all right, I suppose, for the daughters of shopkeepers. By Liverpool standards, yes, it's as good as you'll get. What a lovely afternoon, Frank!'

Gloria was delighted with her Morgan Plus Eight, ordered three years before, and the joy of driving a beautifully engineered sports car finished to her personal specification reconciled her to a journey and a mission in which she had very little interest.

'I'm looking forward to meeting Norah Blanchard,' she conceded. 'From what Mark and Sarah Nolan told us in London that time, she sounds like one of those beads-and-tweeds Englishwomen who vanished into the jungle in Victorian times with half a dozen bearers and a supply of Marmite and came out at the other end six weeks later with a priceless collection of butterflies. People like that are usually good fun, nicht wahr?'

'Jahwöhl, gnädige Frau! Which reminds me, dear Gloria, we haven't done our German practice today. Shall we now?'

'Oh, tomorrow, Frankie. I'm too pleased with life at the moment. You've got to be sad to want to learn things.'

'And here's something more about Norah,' Frank said, consulting his notebook. 'According to Mark this morning, she's Irish, not English, prefers dogs and horses to people, plays bridge and - listen to this! - taught music and French at Rose Choir before she married. How d'you like that?'

His smile faded when he turned to look at Gloria's profile. She was staring rigidly ahead as if at something that frightened her.

Chapter Seven

Because it was premature, Kitty's baby was born before Mrs Osborne returned to Burnett Road. Within hours of discovering that Charles Dooley was her landlord, she had packed a case and left for Wales, there to reside with 'our Flo' until she found a permanent address for herself. 'I'll never forgive that man for what he did as long as I live,' she promised Kitty, and she never did. Facing Dooley after going upstairs to see the baby, she told him grimly: 'I've come back to be with my daughter while she needs me and that's all. If you choose to put me out, so be it. I'll find lodgings nearby.'

'Connie, love! What's the problem? This is your home. Kit wants you and I want you. You should never have walked out on us,' Dooley protested, his cockney voice rising from its normal bluster to a thin whine. 'Take your things off, girl, and join the celebration. Kit's coming down for supper.'

He was preparing roast lamb and vegetables at the new electric cooker, wearing a chef's tall hat and Kitty's frilly pinafore.

'Your room is just as you left it, sweetness. Kit's kept it clean and aired. All that's changed is we're camping out in the lounge while the living room's being gutted. That's all.'

The lounge had been transformed from a cold and dismal room to one that was cheerful and, like the rest of the house, centrally heated. Chintz curtains and a matching Axminster reflected Kitty's preferences, as did the glossy furniture and the three-piece suite in soft black leather. The walls were pale pink, the tiled fireplace oatmeal, the door and skirting boards stripped to expose the original pine. There was a bow-fronted cocktail cabinet, internally lit, a colour television with the biggest screen available and a new wing chair and foot stool, both in gold brocade, to replace the sawn-off sentrybox.

'It had to go, Mum: it was only firewood,' Kitty reasoned, while dressing.

'Firewood! May God forgive you! I nursed you and poor dear Donald in that chair. And what's this you said over the telephone about Roddy and Sooty? What else has he done while my back was turned?'

'They had to be put to sleep and I side with Charles over that. You know what Roddy was like, licking himself all the time, and Sooty was doing his business behind the sideboard. Clare and Nick Pound have taken the hamster and the parakeet.'

'He'd put me to sleep too if he thought he could get away with it,' Mrs Osborne declared, bitterly.

'Charles likes you, Mother. Believe me. He laughs and calls you an original. We cleared the pets out because of Miranda. They could have been carrying something that might be harmful, even fatal, to a new-born child.'

Miranda had been delivered expertly and at home by little old Nurse Dowd, hunchbacked and cackle-voiced, and for three days Kitty had lain with the baby at her side, just smiling at her. Clare and Nick, when visiting, had agreed to be Miranda's godparents, although socialising between the couples had faded away after it became plain that the men didn't like each other. There were moments when it seemed to Kitty that she was alone in liking Dooley.

'You've done so much for me,' she told him, quietly, when she was downstairs. 'And now Miranda. The present I've always longed for. Thank you, Charles.'

'All part of the service,' Dooley replied, as Connie brought the baby into the lounge and carefully placed her among cushions on the sofa.

He was enthroned at the head of the table, waiting for the women to take their places, his white napkin tucked into his collar, his knife and fork held vertically in his clenched fists, one to each side of his place setting. While Kitty ladled celery soup into three bowls, his eyes made a benign survey of the food that lay waiting to be devoured: the tureen of steaming boiled potatoes, the orange carrots and green peas, the large loaf on its cutting board, and the roast leg of lamb that he would shortly stand up to carve. In the course of a week at home, he had proved himself an admirable cook and domestic manager, but this Sunday supper was his swan song, marking the end of his self-imposed housekeeping.

'Where are you off to in the morning, Chummy?' Kitty asked, forgetting in her happiness that Dooley would no more reveal his plans than he would his salary or the amounts of the bills he promptly settled by cheque and with a flourish of his pen. 'Somewhere nice?'

'Nowhere I can take you, my queen.'

'Remember that lovely car I told you about?' Kitty went on, with an amused squeak in her voice. 'I saw it in the road again yesterday, parked with someone in it outside the hod carrier's house. It's an Oxford. Are they good cars?'

'Morris Oxford? All right as cars go, I s'pose. Not as sturdy as the old Cit. She's built like a tank.'

'More modern though, Chummy, and more of a family car. I'd like one in navy blue with light blue inside.'

'You always did like blue, Cath, even when you were small,' Mrs Osborne recalled. 'It's your colour.'

Kitty said: 'The Cit always reminds me of a German sausage dog, doesn't it you, Mum? Will you be away all next week, Chummy?'

She was watching him top up the three wine glasses.

'I'll ring you when I'm on my way home, like I always do,' he answered.

Sometimes he returned without notice and always he wanted to know how Kitty had been spending her time and whom she had seen and spoken with. Until she became too big, he had taken her to a club every Saturday night and for a drive every Sunday afternoon.

'Cath tells me you don't intend charging me any rent for living here,' Mrs Osborne said, when they were finished with the lamb and starting on their peaches and cream. She spoke softly, expressionlessly and without looking up. 'It's kind of you, but if I'm going to stay I want to pay my rent as though nothing had happened.'

'Oh, Mother! Mother, don't be silly!' Kitty protested. 'Charles wants you, not your money.'

'Keep it in your stocking top, Connie,' Dooley advised, 'and let's hear no more about it. We shall proceed now, friends, to wet the baby's head with Armagnac, if I pronounce it correctly. Kit?'

Kitty laughed and said: 'Don't ask me. I don't even know what it is. D'you, Mum?'

'Armagnac is a choice brandy,' Dooley explained, fondling the bottle before opening it. 'And a choice brandy calls for a choice cigar. Have you never smoked, Connie? Never in your life?'

'With my cough? I'd be asking for trouble,' Connie answered.

'Nurse Dowd told me I'd be better without cigarettes,' Kitty confessed, lighting one from Dooley's match. 'She said women who smoke have premature babies and she was right, wasn't she? But I do like a fag, especially after a nice meal.'

'Miranda couldn't wait to have her first look at the world. And I couldn't wait to hold her, could I, Kit?' said Charles. 'What did my boss in London say to me two weeks ago? Polishing his glasses on his tie, he said "Charles! Holding your child in your arms for the first time is an experience you'll never forget". Here's to Miss Miranda Dooley! Bless her and bless her mum.'

'Ah . . .' said Kitty, raising her glass and smiling fondly at Charles. 'That was nice, Chummy.'

'Bless the three of you,' Connie managed, deep in her throat and with downcast eyes.

They drank.

'Now for some photographs,' Dooley proposed, getting up from the table and taking his camera off the mantelpiece. 'I shall have them developed while I'm away and ready for inspection on Friday.'

'Oh, not me, if you please!' protested Mrs Osborne. 'I always look half-witted, don't I, Cath?'

'The camera never lies, Connie,' Dooley told her, with

more brio than tact. 'Miranda has obliged by waking up: so, Connie, when it comes your turn, hold her in your lap and look down at her.'

'You go first, Mum, and sit in your nice new chair,' Kitty urged.

'Oh, all right. Anything to keep the peace. I suppose the sooner I start sitting in it the sooner I'll get used to it.'

Dooley guffawed.

'That's my girl!' he chortled. 'And don't sound so grateful, Connie.'

With the worst will in the world, she had to concede that it was a handsome and comfortable piece of furniture. The seat was higher and firmer than that of the sawn-off sentrybox and there were no loose cushions under which to keep her newspapers. Instead, she had one tucked down behind her, spitting into a torn-off scrap at the end of a bout of coughing, then scrutinising the deposit like a thrifty shopper checking her change before committing it to the fire. Neither Doctor Kinaird's prescriptions nor the many patent medicines she had tried could banish that persistent and deep-seated cough that had plagued her since she was seven.

Even after the newly-decorated living room was back in use, Mrs Osborne continued to sit in her chair in the lounge window, especially during the light evenings, watching the comings and goings in quiet Burnett Road through Kitty's crisp net curtains, sometimes talking to herself, sometimes singing tiddle-omma-tiddle-omma-tiddle-omma-tay. And it was during these solitary watches, after smarting eyes had obliged her to lay aside her library book, that she made two interesting discoveries.

2

It was Dooley's pleasure to return home late on Friday afternoon, to put his arm round Kitty's waist and receive her kiss on his cheek, and then to make much of Miranda, cradling the mite on his left arm, playing with her toes and telling her she was his fairy. There was a little present for her every week, as well as one for Kitty and for Mrs Osborne.

'Ee yar,' he would sneer, handing them out. 'Doan arsk me why I bovver. Ya not werf it, neever of ya.'

Feigned contempt of this kind, immediately softened by a sniff and his sizzling giggle, prevented Mrs Osborne from ever getting to like the man. 'I don't know what it is about Londoners,' she would complain to Kitty. 'They have their own way of saying things. It's as if they mean what they say and yet don't mean it, and it doesn't suit me.'

There was no ambiguity, however, in Dooley's comments on the air raids of the Second World War and still less in Connie's infuriated reaction to them. When he claimed after dinner one night that 'You didn't get no bombin' in the norf. Nah! Not like dear ole L-a-n-don. Land mines. Doodle Bugs. You never got none o' them. Not where you was', Mrs Osborne retorted: 'Is that so? I lost my only son, eleven years old, in the thick of the May blitz, when the sky over Liverpool was red night after night, when the All Clear didn't sound till dawn and my husband risked being drowned in his engine room every time he worked a night shift. So don't you talk to me about bombing.'

She rose from the table, scowling and close to tears, and told Kitty she was 'going up'.

'I'm sorry, Connie, truly I am. Sit down and finish your wine,' Dooley said. 'It's only nine o'clock, sweetness.'

Ignoring him, Mrs Osborne went to the kitchen, then reappeared for a moment in the open doorway, her glass of water in one hand, a folded newspaper under her arm.

'I'll see you in the morning, Cath,' she muttered, playing the aggrieved party to perfection. 'Will you close the door?'

Charles was mopping the whole of his large and now red face with his napkin. He did this at the end of every meal, always reminding Kitty of a cat using one paw for the same purpose.

He was visibly shaken.

'Blimey! Yours Truly has been shot down in flames. I forgot you 'ad a bravver, Kit.'

'Donald. Mum hardly ever mentions him. Never mind. I'll slip up and see she's all right in a minute. Let's sit in front of the fire, Chummy.'

This had become their favourite spot in the refurbished living room after Connie had retired for the night. Sitting side by side on the rust Listerlama hearthrug, holding hands and resting their backs against the sofa, they would finish the wine Dooley had bought on his way home and talk about the week's happenings.

Charles was as well-travelled as a coin of the realm and Cath enjoyed listening to his adventures and to details of his early life. His mother had died in a shop fire when he was still at school, leaving his father to bring him up. Soon after the outbreak of war, at the age of seventeen, he had enlisted in the Royal Engineers, later being transferred to the REME. By then he was a qualified electrician, like his father, who spent his entire working life on the London Underground, starting as an apprentice on the Baker Street & Waterloo Railway, which later became the Bakerloo Line. Dooley's reticence on the subject of girlfriends suggested that his conquests had been few.

'The good lord was keeping me for you, I shouldn't wonder, though I don't know what I done to deserve such a fate.'

'Chummy!'

'Maybe I should've left you in Gravestone Bay with Mr Prompt & Proper.'

'I hope you don't mean that.'

Charles sniggered.

'With that boring bloke? Course not. What d'you suppose he's doing now, Kit? Writing out his toilet roll order or cleaning the reps' shoes for tomorrow morning?'

'Frank's a gentleman of leisure, old boy. The hotel's sold. He's living with a married woman.'

'Perhaps he's not so boring after all.'

'He keeps in touch with Mum.'

'He wants you back, Kit.'

'He's had that.'

'Happy, my queen?'

'Very. Are you? That's more important.'

'You'll be the first to hear about it when I'm not.'

Dooley's Saturday routine was similar to the one he had followed in Birmingham. Between breakfast and dressing for the street, he completed his weekly report and expenses claim, sealed both into a company envelope and posted it on his way to a lunchtime session with 'the blokes' at the Knight of Malta. For them, Saturday was the morning of the chunky sweater and the big wave, the morning when they hailed each other across the car park, the morning when they greeted new arrivals in the Smoke Room (men only) with cries of 'That'll be all!' or 'It's all right for you', without ever specifying what it was that was all right. Next morning, the same hearties, at their respective homes now, would wash and polish the car with the radio blaring and everything on hinges wide open.

Mrs Osborne, from her wing chair, would coldly observe Charles's Saturday departure from behind the net curtains. Always Kitty went outside with him, her arms folded beneath her neat bust, a cigarette burning between her fingers, her squeaky voice and easy laughter belying her antipathy to the old Cit. Couldn't Chummy see it was 'antwacky'? Besides, with his fairy on her arm, she was finding it awkward to get in and out of.

Turning back to the red-and-cream house, she paused to look again at the plaque, no bigger than a twelve-inch ruler, that Charles had had made and that he had earlier fixed to one of the two granite gate posts. Her amused admiration of his boldness, his initiative, his self-confidence, would not, she knew, be shared by her mother when the latter discovered that the house she had entered as a bride was now THE CHARLES DOOLEY RESIDENCE. 'Cheek!' she would certainly exclaim. 'Who does he think he is, for God's sake?'

Kitty joined her at the lounge window, separated from the pavement by a three-foot-high privet hedge and then a low wall.

'Charles looks nice, doesn't he, in casual clothes?' she said, smiling. 'I'm going to buy him a black leather tie for his birthday. He'll wear it if I say it's from Miranda.'

'Has he finished turning the house upside down?'

'There isn't much left to do. Just odds and sods, as Chummy says.'

Mrs Osborne turned her head away and closed her eyes for a moment.

'I love my all-electric kitchen,' Kitty said. 'When you think what it was like before! Oh, look, Mum! There's that Oxford car again – the one I saw outside the hod carrier's, only this time it's on the other side and there's a woman behind the steering wheel.'

'Last time it was a man and the time before it was the same woman as today but in a different car. D'you want my honest opinion, Cath? Dooley's having you watched.'

'Me!'

'Well, who else is there?'

Kitty laughed.

'Why would Charles want me watched?' she asked, flattered.

'Because he knows his own tricks best. How do you know what he gets up to when he's away all week?'

'I don't think I mind, Mum, what he gets up to so long as he's good to me and the little one. Anyhow, there goes your boyfriend from opposite – off to The Brown Penny, no doubt, for his midday pot of beer. I've found out his name, by the way. Michael O'Hanlon.'

3

Some time later, Mrs Osborne returned to the subject of the two cars, this time demanding: 'D'you mean to tell me you haven't tackled him over it?'

'What's the point? They're not there now, are they?' Kitty asked. 'And what if they were? We've got no proof it's our house they're watching or if they're watching any. It may all be just our imaginings.'

But she guessed it wasn't, just as she had guessed that Dooley had someone watching her when they lived in Birmingham. When she had laughingly broached the subject then, Charles had turned away from her in silence and she knew he would do likewise if she revived it now.

Dooley believed not only that women belonged in the background, but that only there could they find happiness and fulfilment. A woman's strength, he claimed, was in her tenderness. Nursing, catering, teaching and caring were the functions for which Nature intended her. These apart, there was nothing she could do that a man couldn't do as well if not better. When she took a job traditionally identified with a man, she trivialised it, making it not worth doing in his eyes.

'Women have invented nothing except marriage,' he would inform 'the blokes' in the safety of the Smoke Room, 'and that's the biggest con trick of all time. Everything they use, from a motor car to a pair of scissors, has been invented by a man.'

Dooley felt threatened by their increasing freedom and mobility, consoling himself with the awareness that the further women encroached on male territory the more they tended to ape men in everything from clothes to expletives. He wondered if they realised that their policy of Look, Listen & Copy illustrated the aphorism that imitation is the sincerest form of flattery. The Samantha who called herself Sam, like the Charlotte who preferred Charley and the woman who wanted to be chairman, was merely confirming male superiority.

'But try calling a man a spokeswoman and watch the feathers fly,' said Dooley, between pints. 'Any suggestion that a man is a woman is an insult. You've devalued him.'

Although his feminine streak made him attractive to women, his fear of them had kept him chaste until well into his maturity. His sexual urge could be pacified quickly, agreeably and without expense by taking himself in hand. In an ideal world, he would have been able to send for a girl from the village. Not until Mary Singleton, and then Kitty Hatfield, had his thoughts turned to marriage in a constructive way.

Even now, Dooley found male company safer and more rewarding than female. Aside from the most primitive of them, whose conversation was confined to 'skirt' and football, he could usually learn from men. They were handier than women, more versatile than women, and more catholic in their sports and pastimes. A man might have a model railway in the garage, an absorbing collection of lichens or an old motor vehicle to restore. He might be a devoted angler, a train spotter in all weathers, or a pigeon fancier, as Kitty's father had been. A woman's pastimes, where they exist at all, are likely to be such as to make a contribution to the home, like needlework or making preserves.

'Women don't get time for anything else,' Kitty pointed out. 'When a man comes home, he does what he wants. When a woman comes home, she does what she must.'

Hotel experience had made her quick and resourceful about the house, whilst her instinct, supplemented by Mrs Osborne's advice, had made her a sensitive and efficient mother. She still wore her engagement and wedding rings but called herself Mrs Dooley in anticipation of her divorce becoming absolute. It was Kitty's pleasure meanwhile to devote herself to her 'husband' and their child, to see that both were well-fed and properly turned out, and to tell herself every now and then that their happiness was all her doing.

Dooley continued to buy every item of Kitty's clothing, and even the outraged Mrs Osborne had to agree, albeit tacitly, that he showed an uncanny flair in deciding what was right for her. Kitty's only stipulation was that her skirts must be knee-length or longer now that she was a mother. She never risked wearing trousers in case Dooley arrived home unexpectedly, which he did at frequent but irregular intervals. She wasn't frightened of her man, although she found it sexually arousing to pretend to herself that she was. Dooley wouldn't raise hand or voice to any female. He showed displeasure either by silence or by a departure as sudden as it was unexpected. One minute he was there, the next he was gone, leaving Kitty with no idea of when he would return or if he would return at all.

He was proud of his queen, proud of his fairy, and proud of himself; since he rejoiced in the common belief that to sire a girl is proof of masculinity.

Every Saturday night, the couple dressed up in their modern evening finery and set out after dinner for the Melody Inn Club in Wallasey Village, leaving Miranda in the care of Mrs Osborne. Dooley's latest purchase for his queen was an ankle-length pencil slim confection in gold charmeuse, slit to the knee and worn with strappy gold shoes with high heels, a gold clutch bag, and long jet beads to match her hair. She danced with Jackson Earle and later Roy Hornby, joint owners of the club, and Charles introduced her to Ralph Cannan, who was there with his wife and from whom he had just bought a nearly-new Morris Oxford.

If Dooley came home during the week, they might go to the pictures, returning with fish and chips for three. Elvis Presley movies were not to be missed, but otherwise they shared no special favourites. Kitty wouldn't go to see an Ingrid Bergman film after discovering that Charles fancied her. She said Ingrid was plain, like a bean pole and had long feet and she couldn't understand what any man saw in her.

She was surprised and gratified when her mother finally consented to accompany them and Miranda on a Sunday afternoon drive. Without telling her, Dooley drove to Lilford Avenue, Fox Hill, stopping outside the house in which she had been born in 1910.

'There you are, sweetness,' he announced, in his cockney whine. 'Drink your fill. They've even left the front door open for you to see inside.'

'I went to my wedding from that house, Cath,' she said. 'Your father and I were married round the corner in Northfield Road.'

'We'll go and see if the church survived the air raids, Connie,' Dooley told her.

'P'raps the bells'll ring again for you, Mum,' Kitty chortled. 'Stranger things have happened, Connie O'Hanlon.'

'Some hopes. Who said I want to marry again anyway? And what makes you think he wants to take the plunge at his time of life?'

'Want me to ask Michael over for Sunday lunch, Connie?' Dooley asked. 'After all, he found me a buyer for the old Cit.'

'Oh yes, Mum! Let's see what he's like,' said Kitty.

Connie said: 'I'll think about it, Charles.'

It was the first time she'd used his name.

Chapter Eight

Norah Blanchard's reaction to Frank's request for an interview gave Gloria the excuse she needed for avoiding a meeting with the woman who may have been a mistress at Rose Choir School when she was a boarder there. Her indignation was nonetheless fulsome and genuine.

'Of all the nerve!' she exclaimed, over a late breakfast at the Station Hotel in Wall Town. 'I'm damned if *I'll* sit in the kitchen with her housekeeper till she gets back from her fox hunting. You can go on your own. I'll drive you as far as the gate and you can ring up here when you want me to come and fetch you.'

'I'll walk there and back.'

'Walk!'

'It's only about three miles to Arrowcross and I need exercise. When I had the New Leaf Hotel, I used to jog every morning, swim at the Ninian and run a weekly keep-fit class.'

'We still swim at the Ninian, don't we? This hotel has been nicely refurbished,' Gloria remarked, looking round, 'but I wish I could get the smell of fresh paint out of my nostrils.'

'Go for a spin in your smart new Morgan while I'm being patronised by Norah Blanchard.'

'I don't want to drive round on my own. I've already driven through enough hamlets with names like Little Clitoris and Constant Farting to last me the rest of my life. I'll just stay here and eat my nails.'

'Don't drink, love, will you? A glass of wine with lunch, then lay off till dinner.'

Gloria was silent for a moment, lighting a cigarette and finishing her coffee. She asked how long Frank expected to spend at Arrowcross Farm.

'Depends how much time Norah Blanchard's willing to give me. Not long, if her attitude over the phone is any indication. At first, she refused to see me.'

'Remind me of where she fits into the picture.'

'She's Robin Blanchard's stepmother. Does that make her Dorothy's mother-in-law?'

'For all practical purposes.'

'I want her to tell me what she remembers about my sister and where to find Robin and, ideally, this Ida Prince, who was Dorothy's secretary at the Willow Square house and who cleared off with Robin shortly before Dorothy's death.'

'What are we going to do between now and luncheon?' Gloria asked. 'Fancy a look at Andover, or would you rather not be reminded of your time in the RAF?'

Frank smiled at her and placed his hand over hers.

'I'm afraid I'll have to read while you drive,' he said. 'A chore for me and a bore for you, but that wire from Neen Savage the Fourth that Mavis read to me over the phone last night is pressing me for a first draft of the biography.'

Gloria sighed and asked how many more of Dorothy's novels remained to be read.

'Three.'

'I suspect you're more conscientious than all but the best of biographers. Must you wade through them all?'

'If I'm to do a proper job.'

'I should think one novel is much the same as another in Dorothy's case. That agent of hers, Mark Nolan, said she wrote strictly for money.'

'It's formula stuff, to be sure. There's no depth, no development. But that's true of the majority of women novelists, whether they write for children or adults. They mature early and thereafter there's no progression.'

'Women are compromised by their major role in reproduction,' Gloria said. 'It's our blessing and our curse. It leaves us in the middle while men occupy the extremes of wickedness and creativity. There's never been a female Hitler or

Michelangelo and there never will be. Come on! Let's enjoy the good weather while it lasts.'

Sight of Andover Staff College, where he had spent most of his National Service engaged in menial tasks, set Frank's thoughts adrift among memories of his early life. Against the wishes of his father, who had entreated him to stay and get his School Certificate, Frank had left Mariner's College at the age of sixteen. His father had wanted him to become articled to a Liverpool firm of architects: instead, Frank insisted on starting a five-year apprenticeship at Doxon Brothers & Caskett, locomotive builders and repairers. He liked to tell the girlfriends he made at Chantry's Dancing School that he was serving his time as an engineer, whereas in reality he was training to be a fitter. The engineers, as his father had tried to tell him, were located away from the erecting and repair shops, away from the dirt and noise, in offices clean and temperate enough to allow them to use their slide rules with their coats over the backs of their chairs and the cuffs of their white shirts turned back.

Within weeks, Frank had begun to envy them their clean clothes and salaried status and within months he had had enough of early rising and the cold and heavy work that filled the eight-hour day. He decided to do his National Service at the age of eighteen instead of seeking the deferment to which, as an apprentice, he was entitled.

He said nothing of this at home until he had been accepted for service with the RAF. By then, he had abandoned the night classes that were a requirement of his apprenticeship, and now, in the time that remained before his call-up, he started taking days off work.

It was a glorious summer. Frank developed a routine. He continued to meet Andy Radstock at a quarter-to-seven five mornings a week at the Dingle terminus of the Overhead Railway; but on Mondays and Fridays, instead of rumbling all the way to the station nearest Doxon's, Frank would part from his friend and fellow-apprentice at James Street and from there take the Mersey Railway to Wallasey Village, where he was unlikely to meet anyone who knew him.

He was free now for the rest of the day: free to walk

through narrow, meandering Wallasey Village in the direction of Harrison Drive and the promenade. He liked the individual shops, the sagging cottages and terrace houses that gave character to the older part of the village between Leasowe Road and Sandy Lane; liked Pear Tree Farm and Big Yard and the early morning scent of new carrots and spring onions that came off market gardens owned and worked by village families. And he liked no less the cool, damp smell of beer through the open door of The Farmer's Arms, where a kneeling woman scrubbed the linoleum, a galvanised bucket at her side and the tops of her stockings coming into view when she reached forward.

Developers would presently arrive to straighten the road, build over the market gardens and replace all that was old and beguiling with uniform dwellings, as neat as they were nondescript. These would symbolise the mass production that was spreading sameness throughout the western world, a sameness that would become evident in everything from cars to clothes, from railway carriages to domestic appliances, so that in time, with individuality swept away, we wouldn't know whether we were in Stockholm or Stockport.

But no such thoughts entered Frank Hatfield's head in that golden summer of 1950, when he made his way to the promenade, when the morning was still new and the human face rare enough to be welcome. Walking towards New Brighton, he had the warmth of the sun on his back and to his side the glittering sea. At low water, he would stand on the foreshore to gaze up at the lighthouse and think how wonderful it would be to live there on his own, with no work to do and nothing to disturb his reverie save the pounding of waves and the call of circling gulls. The Mersey Estuary in those days was alive with dredgers and cargo vessels, drifters and ocean liners, making the youthful truant dream of a life at sea. He saw himself admired by the girls in his officer's navy and gold, with eighty pounds a month and all found, and lots of exotic places to see and write home about.

Businesses had opened by the time Frank turned right opposite the pier and landing stage to walk up Victoria Road, with its numerous shops and amusement arcades, its half dozen pubs and two cinemas, the Court and the Trocadero. Given a wet afternoon, he would retreat into one or other of these, but fine weather found him walking through quiet residential roads to the Derby Bathing Pool, there to spend the rest of the day swimming, eating chocolate, sunbathing and listening to Bunny Berigan playing and singing his favourite *I Can't Get Started* through the loudspeakers.

Despite the tropical suntan he brought home, neither his mother nor his father nor sharp-eyed Dorothy guessed that Frank was taking days off. Every Friday, he made up the shortfall in his wages – twenty-eight shillings for a full week – with cash drawn from the Post Office Savings account that his mother had started for him some two years earlier. He was in the RAF before this was exhausted.

Gloria took her eyes off the road for a moment to smile contemptuously at him. They were nearing Wall Town and Frank had been lost in thought since leaving Andover.

'You never dreamt then, did you, that life could be like this?' she asked, nettled as much by his abstraction as by his unforced entry into her world of money and sophistication.

'No, I don't suppose I did,' he replied.

'It's a far cry from making officers' beds and saluting everyone short of the commissionaire outside the Odeon.'

'The only bed I ever made was my own. I wasn't a batman.'

'Somewhere along the way, you managed to get rid of your Liverpool accent. It used to be pretty thick. I recall your father criticising you over it.'

'I deplore all accents except educated Scots. I have a man called Adrian Hamilton to thank for where I am today,' Frank pointed out. 'He left half his money to me and half to Clare, my first wife. I used mine to pay cash for the New Leaf Hotel and I've just sold it at a handsome profit. It's lunch time. Are you fussy about going back to the Station Hotel or d'you fancy trying this place that's coming up on our left?'

'Why not? It looks recent enough to have running water.'

It was called Bytheway House Hotel.

2

Norah Blanchard was a little tub of a woman, rising seventy, with insufficient hair dyed black, and traces of lipstick on her front upper teeth. Star-bright eyes and a cultured voice with a soft Donegal brogue were her salient features. Dorothy had called her The Poisonous Dwarf. Certainly her legs were short – so short that she would have been more in control riding side-saddle than astride.

She came into her kitchen wearing brown leather ankle boots, fawn jodhpurs, and a dark blue jacket adorned with the buttons and collar patches of the Arrowcross Hunt. Frank rose and waited, but she walked past him and through another door with neither glance nor greeting. He had been waiting an hour. On her way, she told her housekeeper to put the kettle on.

Frank sat down again.

'Starting to rain,' he announced, looking through the open door and across the cobbled yard to a long low stable block with a clock tower on its roof. In the middle distance stood the grey Range Rover that had brought Norah home from the chase. At its rear, the girl driver was about to decouple it from a two-horse box. 'Have you worked here long, Peggy?'

The housekeeper, standing at the Aga cooker with her back to Frank, was slow to answer. He wondered if she resented his calling her by her first name, supplied over the telephone by Norah, or whether he was witnessing a villager's wariness of strangers. She was about thirty, slim and unmarried, wearing brown sandles with ankle socks, a white housecoat and a green snood. Going about her work without offering him any refreshment, she had kept herself to herself. She gave the impression that life had let her down. Perhaps it had. Or was it that Norah Blanchard had cautioned her to say nothing to the visitor?

'I started housekeeping when Mrs Trapnell retired,' she said, opening up a little now that her employer was home and in charge. 'Before that, I only came when they had parties.'

'Did you ever meet my sister? Dorothy Blanchard?'

Peggy hesitated. Then: 'I believe I saw Miss Dorothy just the once – one Christmastime.'

'Once was enough for most people. And Robin Blanchard? Does he ever come here?'

'I think you'd better ask Mrs Blanchard. She'll be down in a moment. I'm going to close this door because the rain's coming in.'

The kitchen had room and to spare for the Aga, for a refrigerator the size of a telephone box, for deep sinks and ample work surfaces, for a Welsh dresser and a scrubbed rectangular table capable of seating twelve adults, six a side, on matching wooden forms. Until mechanisation had put them out of work, farm labourers had been served their meals at this table, summoned from the fields by the clapperbell that still hung outside the kitchen door. The stone floor beneath the table was worn away where their hobnail boots had rested and fidgeted.

After sitting on one of the forms for approaching ninety minutes, Frank's buttocks felt as though transformed into fleshless stumps. He was glad to rise when Norah came back into the room, but she still ignored him.

'I'm sorry my wife isn't with me,' he told the back of her head. 'She has a stomach upset.'

'If Ronnie arrives with the straw and I'm upstairs, call me. I want to see him,' she said to Peggy. 'Prepare dinner for three. Arran and Blanch are coming.'

She was making herself a mug of Maxwell House with hot water from the kettle. She had removed her boots and now she padded across heather matting in thick-knit socks to sit at the opposite end of the table from where Frank had again sat down.

He began: 'It's kind of you to—'

'Ginger pudding for dessert, Peggy,' Norah said. 'Add a dash of brandy to the mix.'

She sipped her coffee.

'How did you get here?' she asked Frank, without looking at him.

'Walked. Not perhaps the best idea I've ever had. Look at—'

'I'm meeting you out of curiosity, not out of fondness for your sister,' Norah said. 'Your sister was beautiful in a cold way and nasty in every other. She was a social climber who married my stepson, Robin, because she could see no other way of escaping one room in Belsize Park. She had no feeling for him or for anyone else. People existed to be used and then dropped.'

Peggy, moving between cooker and fridge, gave her employer a worried look, as though fearing an outburst of violent or irrational behaviour.

Frank said, thinking to ingratiate himself: 'What you say doesn't entirely surp—'

'She used to beat Robin if she couldn't get what she wanted and he was too good and too kind to do more than try to defend himself and reason with her,' Norah continued, still sipping and staring now at the Welsh dresser. 'His daughter, Hilary, who came to live here because she couldn't bear her stepmother, told me what went on at Willow Square. Your sister was a selfish and sadistic woman. Put that in your notebook. She was never welcome at Arrowcross, I can tell you that. Tomato soup tonight, Peggy, with croutons. Robin is as saintly a spirit as you'll find in this world and your sister made his life a misery.'

'Why?'

'Frustration. Disappointment. She wanted to be a respected novelist, like her heroine Cynthia Justin Bourn, but all she was capable of was adventure stories for schoolgirls.'

'Robin could have left her,' Frank reasoned.

'Robin can't cope with life on his own. In the end, of course, he did leave her to start a new life with her secretary, Ida Prince, and Ida has made him very happy. He stayed with your sister because, until his father died, she alone had the money to send Hilary to Rose Choir School and to maintain her there.'

'So there was some good in Dorothy after all. She didn't live exclusively for herself.'

When Norah made no answer, Frank asked her if he might use her telephone to order a taxi.

'Our telephone is out of order,' she replied, before he had finished speaking. 'You'll have to walk to the house at the end of the drive and ask Arran or Blanch Clark if they'll let you use theirs.'

Watching the heavy rain beyond the windows, Frank missed the look that Peggy gave the older woman on her return trip from the fridge to the Aga. It blended distress with bewilderment.

'What you should do is talk to Robin and Ida,' Norah said, padding over to one of the twin draining boards with her empty mug. 'You'll find them at Bytheway House Hotel.'

'Gloria and I have just lunched there.'

'Remember to put a bay leaf in with the potatoes, Peggy, and add basil to the soup. I suggest you ring them up first. Robin will talk to anyone. Ida is the brains and a very busy and very lovely woman, and I only wish Rob had married her instead of the other one. It's time for my bath.'

'Would it be possible to talk with Hilary, Mrs Blanchard?'

'You'd have to find her first. They're on a world tour in an old Pickford's removal van and won't be back for months. Hilary married the London architect who came to design the bedroom block at Bytheway House. When Rob and Ida took it, along with another couple – the least said about them the better – it was just a restaurant and not a very good one either.'

Norah walked out of the room, saying as she went: 'Blanch and Arran Clark. Tell them who sent you.'

Frank rose to say goodbye to Peggy. Their eyes met for a moment and hers were full of sympathy.

He was part-way down the drive, walking with his collar turned up and the lapels held together over his tie, when she called to him from the kitchen door.

'Sir! Sir! Camilla will drive you into Wall Town.'

'Oh, all right.'

'Mrs Blanchard says to wait in the stables.'

'Tell her I'll muck-out if she'll lend me a shovel.'

Before dinner that evening, in their suite at the Station Hotel, Frank arranged a meeting with Ida for the next morning. No sooner had he put the telephone down than it rang again. An irate Norah Blanchard was on the line.

'My groom tells me you quizzed her about me and my family when she was driving you back to your hotel,' she snapped.

Frank frowned.

'I don't know about quizzing. I may have—'

'Well, I don't like it and I've already warned Ida about you.'

'I thought your telephone was—'

Norah had hung up.

3

'The more feminine a woman is, the more she resents other women,' Gloria announced, when dressing for their meeting with Ida Prince. 'Men foregather: women don't. There's something wrong with a woman who wants to be with other women.'

'Is that official? You're calling her Ida Prince, by the way. She isn't. She's Ida Blanchard,' Frank corrected, knotting the yellow silk tie that Gloria liked him to wear with his purple shirt, navy blue blazer, light grey trousers and Hush Puppies. 'Ready, Glorious? My, you do look nice! Lavender mini skirt, black silk blouse, ankle-strap high heels *and your diamonds!* Who would ever guess it's a woman you're about to meet?'

Gloria, seated at the dressing table, was putting the finishing touches to her make-up.

'You wouldn't think I was twenty-five, would you?' she asked, turning her head this way and that. 'I mean to say, I don't *look* twenty-five, do I?'

'Oh no, Gloria. You don't look twenty-five.'

'That's what everyone says, so it must be true. My hair looks like a bird's nest. I think she set it with a pair of knitting needles.'

'Why didn't you wait till we get to Exeter, where there may be a Steiner's?'

'My own fault. I got it wet yesterday afternoon, while you were flirting with Norah. How old is this Ida Blanchard?'

'As old as she feels.'

She was forty, which made her a little younger than Gloria and a little older than Frank. Like Neen Savage the Fourth, she kept the couple waiting; but the reception area at Bytheway House Hotel was less austere and more animated than that of Hamilton Jupp Incorporated. Hilary's husband had designed the interior as well as the structure, and his use of softly glowing redwood for the coffered ceiling, of stone cladding in sage green and of rough-cast brick for the wide fireplace showed the influence of Frank Lloyd Wright. Frank Hatfield and Gloria waited in two of the dozen or so tub chairs upholstered in grey suede and standing, like the several matching sofas, on an amber carpet with a diamond trellis design in chocolate brown and a border in the same colour. There were many silk scatter cushions in Aztec patterns, maroon glazed pots and vases overflowing with yellow and tangerine roses, and a score of brown ebony wine tables, each provided with an ashtray and a tall square tower lamp in yellow and pink art glass.

'All this has cost a pretty penny,' Frank mused, guessing correctly that the money had come to Ida from the sale of Dorothy's copyrights.

Bored and ready to be displeased should the opportunity present itself, Gloria was sitting upright, one shapely leg crossed over the other, smoking her third cigarette since breakfast.

'Where is this dame?' she asked, tightly.

'Coming towards us,' Frank murmured.

A moment later, Ida was smiling and apologising and inviting them to follow her into her office.

'Coffee for both of you? I'll have to keep it brief, I'm afraid, and you won't have to mind if my telephone keeps ringing.'

Frank said: 'It's when it stops ringing that your problems start. I used to have a hotel myself, only not in such lovely countryside as this. May I introduce Mrs Raby? She's my friend and helper in the life-story project.'

'Not much of a helper. I know even less about how to go about it than you do,' Gloria responded, moodily.

She eyed with scorn the dog-eared notebook that Frank brought from his pocket and the cheap ball-point pen that followed.

Ida's voice was low and husky, with traces of a north Manchester accent. She said: 'I think Dorothy once mentioned she had a brother, but I can't be sure. She wasn't one for discussing her affairs.'

'Did she ever speak of Gloria Brown? That was Mrs Raby's maiden name and she and my sister were buddies when they were in their teens.'

'I don't recall. It's worth remembering, Mr Hatfield, that I was only an employee. I can tell you most things about Mary Orchard, but next to nothing about Dorothy Blanchard.'

'I'd have to talk with Robin about her, wouldn't I? Is that possible?'

Ida hesitated. Her manner from the outset had been professional, rather distant, and now it became faintly condescending.

'Most things are possible, Mr Hatfield, but not today. My husband is fully occupied preparing a banquet. This will be Arabella with our coffee.'

A slender man of medium build, blue eyed and fair skinned, entered backwards, bearing a laden tray, which he set down on the end of Ida's desk.

'Where is Arabella?' she asked. 'Absent?'

'Gone to the cash and carry,' the man answered. He was dressed in chef's clothing, complete with tall pleated hat. With a smile and a blink for the visitors, he asked who was the proud owner of the Morgan? Could Gloria move it to make way for a delivery van? He'd hate to see such a splendiferous car damaged.

Gloria excused herself, leaving Frank and Ida to smile at one another in silent communion.

'How proud you must be, Mr Hatfield, of your famous sister!' Ida said. 'Dorothy was a genius.'

'I wouldn't go quite that far, Mrs Blanchard.'

'Oh yes! You can't write twenty-odd novels in ten years and not be a genius.'

'They're all out of print.'

'Not in America, Mr Hatfield, where she's having a rebirth. And isn't it true that a genius is never recognised in his own country? Isn't there something in Shakespeare to that effect?'

'Very likely,' Frank said. 'Immortal William had something worthwhile to say on most subjects and sometimes he said it in an unforgettable way. His weaknesses are monumental verbosity, his obsession with blood and madness, those beard-stroking soliloquies and his frequent blossoming into rhyming verse unworthy of a schoolboy. But don't get me going on literature, Mrs Blanchard.'

'Why not? I like what I'm hearing.'

'But you've got things to do.'

'They can wait.'

'I've got nothing.'

'Do you wish it otherwise?'

'More and more.'

They continued to smile at each other. Frank's attention was centred on Ida's moon face, copper coloured hair worn short and straight, the slow smile that lifted her chin slightly, and the most beautiful green eyes under heavy lids. Gloria would later praise them excessively so as to avoid admiring any other aspect of Ida's appearance. No mention would be made of Ida's Nile green tailored two-piece, her tan blouse open over its collar or the exquisite antique cameo that had been a present from Norah Blanchard.

'Norah has been marvellous to me,' Ida said, pouring coffee into three monogramed cups. 'I'd have lost this hotel if she hadn't stepped in to save me. Norah knows people who can make things happen and people who can stop them happening. Norah has friends internationally.'

'Dorothy wasn't one of them.'

'There was a rift between them at some point, Mr Hatfield, but it was before I went to work for your sister and she never referred to it.'

'According to Mark Nolan, it was my sister's attitude to humanity. Some of her ideas were bleak, even brutal, as I remember myself. Dorothy believed the State should supervise procreation, with those considered unfit to breed being sterilised. Norah, I gather, is Roman Catholic.'

'I won't be able to spare you very much more time, Mr Hatfield,' Ida said, quietly.

Her eyes were lowered, her lips sealed. Mark Nolan was someone she had chosen to dislike, at first to his mystification, later to his indifference. Ida had ignored him at Dorothy's funeral, where she was the only woman (in black from head to foot and heavily veiled) among fewer than half a dozen mourners. And now, four years on, she slightly regretted having made an enemy of him. Had Mark acted for her in her hurried negotiations with Hamilton Jupp Incorporated, the sum paid for Dorothy's rights might have been doubled.

Frank was asking if Robin and Dorothy had had any children when Gloria came back into the office and sat down.

Ida said: 'Drink your coffee before it gets cold, Mrs Raby.'

'Your chef liked my car so much, I let him park it for me.'

Ida's smile was tolerant.

'Children?' she resumed, addressing Frank. 'No. Dorothy miscarried. She and Robin were involved in a car crash and Dorothy got the worst of it, as passengers usually do. Your pen is poised for more answers to more questions, Mr Hatfield, but I'm afraid I'm running out of time.'

'Why not lunch with us? Gloria and I have got to eat somewhere and it's nearly one o'clock.'

'Lunch? What's that? If you can call back in the morning, I'll have my recollections of Dorothy typed out ready for you.'

'We're leaving for Exeter in precisely one hour,' Gloria stated, firmly, looking at the small gold watch that was always slipping round her wrist. 'I suggest Mrs Blanchard posts it to you, Frank.'

'But we don't know where we're staying, Gloria, and I need the information quickly. What if we stay the night here, Mrs Blanchard, and will you and Robin dine with us?'

Frank sensed Gloria's rising temper as he hurried to explain to Ida that such an arrangement would complete his research and there would be no need to bother the Blanchards further.

'The hotel is full, Mr Hatfield.'

'It's just one more night, Gloria,' Frank pleaded, turning to her and pressing the small hand that she promptly removed from her thigh. 'We can go back to the Station Hotel, return here tomorrow morning and be on our way by ten.'

Gloria, tight-lipped, neither spoke nor looked at him.

'Would it be possible, Mrs Blanchard, to have a word with Robin in the morning?' he asked, urgently.

Ida rose, her smile once again professional.

'I'll see what I can do,' she promised.

Gloria walked out in disgust, but Frank lingered to clasp Ida's hand, to smile into the green eyes that Dorothy had loved and to thank her.

'It's been my pleasure,' she said, returning his smile and the pressure of his hand. 'I'm glad we've met. Where is Mrs Raby, I wonder?'

'On her way to the car, I suspect. I hope she waits for me.'

'I'm sure she will, Mr Hatfield.'

Gloria was snappy and sulky and mostly silent during luncheon. After two powerful shots of gin and tonic, she went to bed for the afternoon. Frank, who used her absence to get on with some writing in their sitting room, thought it unwise to comment on her drinking or to try to prevent it when it resumed in the evening. Left unchallenged, it would, he believed, return to moderation.

Though still withdrawn, Gloria was brighter next morning, when their cases were again stowed in the Morgan. She waited behind the wheel with the engine running while Frank went inside Bytheway House, and remained staring silently ahead when he got back in beside her, a sealed envelope in his hand.

'No luck with Robin. No luck with either of them,' he said, as Gloria let in the clutch. 'Gone to a wine tasting somewhere.'

He didn't tell Gloria that there had been vacant rooms the night before and she didn't tell him that the chef was Robin Blanchard.

Chapter Nine

To Kitty's amusement and her mother's simulated indifference, Michael O'Hanlon accepted Dooley's invitation to luncheon, duly crossing the road from his lodgings the following Sunday on the dot of the appointed hour, as befitted an old soldier, and bearing flowers for his hostess.

But Kitty acted quickly.

'They're for you, Mum,' she decided, before introducing Mrs Osborne to their guest and leaving them together with: 'Go and sit in the lounge with Mother, Mr O'Hanlon, till lunch is ready and my husband gets back and I'll put the flowers in water and bring them back in a moment.'

By now, Mrs Osborne, from her wing chair behind the net curtains, had grown used to watching for Punch, as Dooley had nicknamed the Ulsterman on account of his impressive nose ('If that geezer stood sideways, you'd think he was sounding the Last Post'), noting that he left for The Brown Penny at precisely noon, returning to the Leylands' at one o'clock, then emerging at three for an afternoon stroll. He drank his pints sitting in the bar, as once Clive Rolls had done, smoked his No Name tobacco, read his *Merseyside Express* and, when appropriate, told people that 'I spent my life in service to a lovely family and they've left me in a position where I need never worry about money again.'

A genial man, he had a long face which, when not divided by one, carried the promise of a smile. His skin was as brown as his eyes, as wrinkled as a prune and without beard or moustache. He usually dressed in a yellow and grey check sports jacket, moleskin trousers, a white corduroy cap pulled down over one eye, and sometimes brown-and-white spectator shoes. His walk was leisurely, left hand in trouser pocket, right hand toying with a stick and occasionally twirling it. There was a day-at-the-races jauntiness about him that appealed to Mrs Osborne.

'I was a chauffeur-handyman,' he explained, over roast pork, roast potatoes, carrots and broccoli, all prepared by Dooley, who, still wearing his chef's hat, presided at the head of the table. 'When I started at Fred's Fields, the family home, the Tadlers had two cars – a Weymann bodied Standard Teignmouth and a big, sturdy Hudson. The Hudson ran best on Cleveland fuel, but the Standard was happier with Pratt's Motor Spirit, sold in two-gallon tins in those days, so I had to go to the local hardware shop for the Pratt's and to a pub in the next village for the Cleveland. But I loved driving, especially continental touring and especially when the Tadlers bought a Rolls-Royce Phantom, which was promptly commandeered by the army in September 1939.'

'Did you serve in the war, Mr O'Hanlon?' Connie asked. 'I expect you did.'

'In the same regiment as Joe Leyland.'

'Your friend,' Kitty said to Dooley, with a squeak of amusement in her voice. 'Chummy's chum.'

After a dispute over parking, Charles and Joe Leyland, whose house faced number 4, hadn't spoken. 'The long streak of piss,' Charles would call out from behind the net curtains if he spotted Joe from the lounge or the front bedroom. He was nearly seven feet tall, exceptionally thin and with a small head. Once, at the Waverton indoor baths, someone had bellowed 'Who threw them braces in?' as Joe surfaced from a dive. He had never gone swimming again.

Leyland was a debt collector, the sight of whom, spluttering round with streaming eyes and fluttering trousers on an old Rudge motorbike, was all too familiar to those who got behind with their payments. His wife, who was known as Muff, seldom emerged without blue plastic rollers in her hair and quilted slippers with pink pompoms on them. If Connie saw her through the window, she would think to herself or say to

Kitty: 'Our Muff. She's going to the corner for her fags and the *Daily Mirror*. Look at her little pot belly and her nose in the air. She can hardly see her hand in front of her, but she won't wear glasses.'

Kitty asked where O'Hanlon's wife was, as they would have liked to invite her too. The Irishman answered that police were digging in the back garden when he left just now, adding, more seriously, that he wasn't blessed in that direction.

'Have you never been married? I'll bet he hasn't,' Dooley wagered, boisterously. 'That's why he always looks chuffed.'

'Chummy!' Kitty protested.

'I took a girl out for three weeks when I was fourteen,' O'Hanlon replied, in his softly caressing voice. 'That was quite sufficient.'

Laughing, Dooley chortled: 'Hey, I like this bloke. He can come again. So how d'you spend your time, Michael, when you're not burying something in the back garden? What d'you do all day, me ole son?'

'Well, we've all heard of the American negro who said "Sometimes I sits and thinks and sometimes I just sits",' O'Hanlon replied. 'I'm like him, sure. Between daily doses of Liffey water, I sit myself down in the reading room at Waverton library for a free look at the news. And what about you, Charles? What keeps you out of mischief when you're not prowling round the Nurses' Home after dark?'

'Who told him?' Dooley thundered. Then: 'Me? I drives and I thinks. I thinks about what our country will be like when the last drop of oil has fallen from the tap.'

'When will that be, Charles? Or haven't you decided yet?' Connie Osborne prompted, sipping her wine.

'Well, it can't be much longer, sweetness, can it? You can't go on sucking an orange without sucking it dry. We're talking decades, not centuries, before our motorways are deserted and overgrown.'

'Nature is the world's number one vandal,' O'Hanlon said. 'She'll wreck anything. Leave your property unattended for a year and she'll turn your garden into a wilderness and be well on the way to dismantling your house.'

'Anyone who wants a secure job in the twenty-first century should start training as a wheelwright, a harness maker or a breeder of heavy horses,' said Dooley.

'But won't there be other fuels?' Connie asked. She was convinced there would be. 'What's this we hear about nuclear energy? I read something the other day to do with a farmer in Devon, I think it was, who runs his car on hen droppings.'

'Methane,' explained O'Hanlon, without pronouncing the h.

Kitty said: 'The police are experimenting with electric cars in some parts of the country.'

Dooley was dismissive.

'Hen muck won't keep a lorry on the road. Electricity won't get a Boeing 707 up there. As for nuclear power, what are we doing to develop it as an alternative to petrol and diesel? We're not even nibbling at the problem. And who's to say the internal combustion engine in its present form will run on nuclear fuel? All our engines may have to be adapted, even scrapped. Tens of millions of them. What then?'

O'Hanlon predicted that the western world would run dry first.

'Oil is only beginning to come on stream in the eastern half,' he said. 'By the time the west is a desert littered with abandoned vehicles, China will have replaced America as the number one world power and India won't be far behind. The pre-eminence of the white man will be over.'

Connie said, with a satisfied chuckle: 'Well, I shall be dead and gone by then.'

'Oh, Mother! Don't talk like that,' Kitty said, genuinely disturbed.

'Why? What's so terrible about dying?' Mrs Osborne wanted to know. 'We welcome sleep: why should we fear death?'

'Sure, we all wish our lives away, Connie,' said smiling O'Hanlon. 'Could that not indicate a subconscious awareness of a better life to come?'

Connie asked him if he read much, knowing he would answer in the affirmative. She used to say she could tell in five minutes if someone was a reader.

'More than ever since I've retired,' he assured her.

'Have you read any of Mulsanne's novels?'

'Not in recent years, Connie. I've read some Colette in my old age and the whole of Proust. In translation, I have to admit. On my last continental tour with the family, we went to look at Colette's birthplace.'

The meal over, Kitty gave Dooley a signal to leave the room with her.

'Mulsanne claimed in his autobiography to despise death,' Mrs Osborne said. 'I can recall what he said. He said that death was so unspeakably common, so depressingly available to all and sundry, irrespective of social standing, that he viewed its approach with contempt.'

'I like his indignation. He clearly felt that death had a nerve picking on him. His vocabulary is reminding me, Connie, of Henry James, who called Bernard Shaw "the unspeakable Irishman". How GBS must have loved that!'

'I've never tried Shaw. One of his plays was on television last week, but I can't get used to television. Charles and our Cath have it on from morning till night, but I'd rather sit in the lounge and read my library book. I'm reading some of Somerset Maugham's short stories at present.'

'Television sedates the mob, sure. Take it away and they'll start demanding the return of bull baiting and public executions. If you can spare an evening next week, why not come with me to see Shaw's *Arms and the Man* at the Liverpool Playhouse?'

'I'd enjoy that. I'm a bit surprised at your liking Shaw though.'

'Why ever d'you say that?'

'You're Catholic, I presume. And Irish. Wasn't Shaw Ireland's naughty boy?'

'I'm a lapsed Catholic, Connie. An old heathen.'

'Funny, isn't it, how people never call themselves lapsed Anglicans or lapsed Quakers or lapsed anything else. Yet how often have we heard the expression "lapsed Catholic"?'

'As to my nationality, sure I'm only half Irish, Connie, which is why I take only the afternoon off on St Patrick's Day. My mother, bless her, was a wee Scots lassie from Cruden Bay.'

2

Even when close to suicide, Kitty had shown the world a happy face, a face that said 'yes!' to life. Now, with a child on her hip and another expected, she was radiant. She had her home, her man, and, with the divorce now absolute, her freedom to marry him.

'Here's your coffee, Connie O'Hanlon,' she squeaked, joyfully, when the hands of the living room clock stood at 11am. 'Are you seeing your boyfriend again tonight?'

With the evenings drawing in and the temperature falling, Charles had carried the wing chair into the living room, placing it with its back to the windows to make reading easier for Connie. Whilst she appreciated central heating, even admitting as much, she still liked to 'see a bit of fire' and this was possible in the living room all the year round. Charles lit a fire in the lounge only at Easter and over Christmas, transferring it on a shovel to the living room before bed.

This room had tender memories for Connie, since it was here that she had nursed and nurtured 'our Cath' and 'poor dear Donald', the only son, who had died in 1941. The boy had become her consolation after Harry Osborne's interest had shifted from her to his pigeons, also her companion on those evenings when Harry was on watch in his engine room and Cath upstairs in bed. They had spoilt themselves with Eccles cakes and Rowntree's cocoa, and Donald, sitting in front of the fire with his knees up to his chin and his back against the front of the sofa, had sung *If I Had My Way* from sheet music bearing a photograph of Bing Crosby on the cover.

It had been the boy's dearest wish to have a clockwork gramophone and start a collection of records, and his mother had promised him one as soon as the war ended and they became available again. Meanwhile, from her broken down armchair in the pool of yellowish light cast by a standard lamp with a red fringed shade, she had read aloud to him, noticing with pleasure how lost he became in *Robinson Crusoe* and such favourite short stories as *Ten Pennies* and *The Knapsack, the Hat and the Horn*.

'He died of meningitis,' she told O'Hanlon. 'Like other

schoolboys during the war, Donald went about collecting shrapnel and cordite and, he told me, swapping the best pieces in the playground. He kept his collection in a biscuit tin in the Anderson air raid shelter in the back garden, where him and his pal, Alec Kelly, used to burn candles and experiment with things they bought at the chemist's – iron filings, I remember, and copper sulphate. I got Harry to see what they were doing, but you can't be watching them all the time.'

Along with other boys, the friends would play in the wreckage of bombed houses, from one of which Donald brought home an unexploded incendiary bomb. He took it into the back garden, where he unscrewed it to see what was inside. It detonated. Had it done so in the confines of the shelter, Donald would have been burnt to death. As it was, the man next door put the fire out with soil and a shovel and Donald suffered only a scolding from his mother and the threat of another from his father.

'You just wait, my lad, till he sees the mess you've made and the fright you've given his birds! Look at them. Flying round like mad things. They think it's the end of the world.'

The pigeons had calmed down and the boy was close to death by the time Harry Osborne joined Connie at their son's bedside.

'Donald complained of tiredness and a headache shortly after I'd given him his tea, so I sent him off to bed, thinking it was delayed shock. About half an hour later, I looked in, expecting to find him asleep. But he was wide awake and sweating and he covered his eyes when I put the light on. I gave him half an aspirin with a sip of water and sat with him; but he started murmuring and having trouble getting his breath. I went next door and used their telephone to speak to Doctor Kinaird's wife.

'The doctor was out on call. By the time he reached us – it was turned nine o'clock – bombs were falling and guns banging and Donald was delirious. His head and spine were drawn backwards like a bow. It wasn't shock and it wasn't the "flu" or even pneumonia, as I'd started to think it might be. "Meningitis", the doctor said, as soon as he had examined him; and it was obvious from the way he spoke and the way he was looking at Donald that the poor kid was in danger.'

While Cath slept in the next room and Harry was walking home from the Pier Head because the buses and trains had stopped running, Connie, from the end of the bed, watched Dr Kinaird strip the writhing boy and sponge his brow and body with cold water.

'Shouldn't he be in hospital, Doctor?' she ventured, with a dry throat. She cleared it. 'Can't they die of meningitis?'

The doctor straightened up, his sad eyes unable for a moment to leave the blue rash that was turning black on the boy's chest. He took Donald's wrist between finger and thumb and found what he expected: the pulse was weakening.

'I'm afraid there's nothing any of us can do, Mrs Osborne, in or out of hospital. Once the rash shows, you must prepare yourself for the worst. I'll stay here and do the little I can to make it easier for him.'

In the early hours of the morning, when all had gone quiet outside, the boy died with his father and mother and Dr Kinaird at his bedside.

Even now, thirty years later, Connie still went to Waverton Cemetery to tidy his grave and leave flowers and wonder how he would have turned out, what career he would have followed and what sort of girl he would have brought home.

'He was Mum's favourite,' Kitty said, without rancour, to Charles Dooley. 'I was my dad's. He used to sit me on his knee by the fire and read *Sunny Stories* to me while Mum got his tea ready, and he'd stand me on the toilet seat when he was shaving to go to work. Mum treated both of us the same, but I was always second best and still am. Sometimes she'll say nasty things to me – things meant to hurt – that I know she'd never say to Donald if he was here today.'

Photographs of 'our Cath' stood on the mantelpiece in lounge and living room alike, but the only one extant of 'poor dear Donald' lay in a drawer of his mother's dressing table, together with a vest he'd worn as a toddler and the little letter he'd sent home from a Scout camp in Market Drayton.

Kitty scarcely remembered her brother, and so her memories associated with the living room at 4, Burnett Road were different from Mrs Osborne's. What she remembered and what she wanted to recreate for her own children was the ambiance of warmth and security that had awaited her return from school. 'Get those wet things off,' she could hear her mother say, 'and put them on the maiden to dry in front of the fire.' Kitty had liked the winter afternoons, the short sharp days and early twilights, the curtains drawn against the wartime blackout, the glowing coke fire and the box of toys that she unloaded onto the hearth rug. Her mother was always there. She was at home to see Kitty off to school in the morning, at home when she returned for her dinner, at home when she came in shortly after four. She remembered her mother kissing her and asking what she'd done at school before they sat down together at the table to have their tea and listen to the Pye radio that had scared the wits out of the cat the first time Harry Osborne had switched it on and found the volume set at full.

'I don't want to go out to work again, Chummy,' she said to Charles. 'A lot of the bad behaviour among today's children is because television is more influential than mum and dad; but it's also because mum isn't at home to ask questions and see who their friends are. I want our children to be good citizens and we can help them by setting the right example. It may mean going without things we could've had if I'd gone back to work, but that's a sacrifice parents should be prepared to make.'

'Well said, my queen. Kids might kid father, but not mother. She's always one jump ahead of them.'

'Not if she comes home tired and has to start all over again with cooking and cleaning and mending. In that kind of family, it's all too easy to give the kids money and tell them to go out and enjoy themselves. I can understand it, but it's not going to happen here.'

'You've got it all worked out, haven't you?'

'That's part of my job as a wife and mother. When I see children walking to school with a bag of crisps and a tin of Coke or dumped at the gates by parents on their way to work, my heart goes out to them. If there's one thing above all that I've got my parents to thank for, it's the fact that they fed and clothed us properly.'

Doing both had called for sacrifice and resourcefulness,

particularly when the Second World War brought ration books, clothing coupons and official exhortations to *Dig for Victory* and *Make Do & Mend*. As a soldier, Dooley had been comparatively well-fed, but civilians had to get through each week on portions of sugar, bacon, butter, tea, lard and cheese that would all fit comfortably on a single dinner plate. Kitty recalled with a smile that they were allowed one egg a week and meat to the value of two shillings.

'Twenty pence in decimal money,' she said, laughing. 'For a special treat now and then, Dad used to take me to one of the British Restaurants that popped up all over the place and where you could get a one-course meal for a shilling. Once he took me across to Wallasey on his ferry boat and we had our dinner at the British Restaurant in Liscard Village.'

Nearby, she had noticed a dress shop called Sonia's. Much later, when in her early twenties and still hoping Clive Rolls would marry her, she had bought a light grey two piece with a brown collar that she saw displayed in the window. Frank Hatfield was with her. Although engaged to Clare Mason, his love for Cathy Osborne had led him to betray Clare's trust and to go on betraying it until her accidental pregnancy put an end to the affair.

On many of their dates, Kitty had worn the two-piece, known as a costume in those days, to please Frank. He liked it not only because it became her, but equally because, while she was trying it on at Sonia's, the manageress had called him Mr Osborne in the belief that the couple were man and wife. Five years on from that day, by which time his marriage to Clare was breaking up and Clive Rolls was dead, Frank had reminded Kitty of the incident when at last he could ask her to marry him. Till then, he claimed, it had been the happiest day of his life.

'He proposed to me in this room,' she told Dooley. 'I said I remembered the incident, but I didn't because I was never really interested in anything to do with Frank. I married him because there was no one else and I didn't want to be left on the shelf.'

Predictably, Charles exclaimed: 'That boring bloke! Just tell me once more what he said to you about two halves, Kit.'

'Oh, that!'

'It's a little classic. Samfink to keep for our grandchildren. Go on.'

'He told me I shouldn't say "two halves" – just "halves" – because you can't have three of them. He meant well. He used to give me his lovely smile and pretend he was wearing glasses and look over them at me and say things like "Don't say 'the very first time'. Leave the 'very' out, because you can't have a very first anything, any more than you can have a very second or a very last anything".'

'Oh, dearie me! The schoolmaster. I shall die laughing one of these days. They call people like him pendants, Kit.'

In ways like this, without ever seeking or intending to do so, Frank had made his Cathy feel intellectually inferior. His knowledge of life, of grammar, of literature, reduced hers to insignificance. But Dooley was on her level, if not below it. Without self-consciousness, Kitty could read *Sweethearts* while Charles read *Macho* and afterwards they could sit hand-in-hand on the living room sofa and enjoy *Coronation Street* or *Emergency Ward Ten*.

3

Their night out was Saturday, when Mrs Osborne stayed with Miranda and Michael O'Hanlon came over at precisely 8pm to sit with her by the living room fire. He always brought with him a bottle of good quality wine, which they drank later with the chicken or salmon sandwiches that Connie had prepared in advance and left under a damp tea towel in the kitchen.

Although she rarely addressed her companion by name, she had started referring to him as Michael instead of the slightly pejorative 'that O'Hanlon'. Dooley, Kitty noticed, was less privileged. He might now be Charles to his face, but he remained Dooley when his back was turned. Connie still brooded in solitude and sour contentment on his cockney whine, his bluster, his overweening self-assurance. He could never replace Frank Hatfield.

'Would you say Dooley was a good driver?' she asked O'Hanlon, stressing the adjective and hoping for adverse criticism.

Her hopes were realised.

'Sure, he's what I call a brakes and throttle driver,' was the Irishman's considered reply. 'Jerky. He only took me to the Knight of Malta and back, but I noticed he didn't use the gears to control his speed. There was no forward planning, if you see what I mean. He wasn't reading the road, as they taught us to do at Rolls-Royce.'

'You trained there, didn't you?'

'When the Tadler family bought their Phantom, they sent me on the chauffeurs' driving course that Rolls-Royce ran in the 1930s. Believe me or believe me not, we spent three days on gear changing alone.'

'Well, of course, being a woman I don't understand such things. We never owned a car. Until the end of the war, the only cars that came into the road were the doctor's and the hearse.'

Smiling O'Hanlon took the pipe out of his mouth to say: 'Not in that order, I hope.'

'My family were what I call best end of lower class. Father was a school attendance superintendent.'

'Mine was an ostler, who never went to school and couldn't read or write. We were bottom end of lower class.'

O'Hanlon senior saw to the welfare of as many as thirty heavy horses owned by several Belfast team owners and housed in stables on the opposite side of Roscommon Street from Rose Gardens, where he lived with his wife, his son and two daughters, one of them epileptic. He was lame, gross in speech and habits, but sober and reliable. Every penny of his earnings and of his wife's went to making ends meet. Mrs O'Hanlon was a charwoman, cleaning the local picture house in the mornings and a solicitor's offices after the close of business. She never stopped work except to sleep and bear children. Her husband spent such free time as the horses allowed sitting by the kitchen range in shirt sleeves and baggy corduroys stiff with dirt, smoking Woodbines, bellowing at the children to make less noise and spitting gobbets of yellow phlegm into the fire, where they fried like eggs among the hot coals or, if his aim were at fault, hissed on the bars until cremated.

Rose Gardens was just big enough to accommodate six terrace houses – three to each side of a stone-flagged court in which numerous children noisily played hopscotch or kick-the-can. A row of water closets, their wooden doors numbered one to six, filled the blind end of the court. The tall, narrow houses were of the two-up-and-two-down variety, each with a coal cellar and stone steps leading up to the front door. Oil lamps downstairs and acrid tallow candles in the bedrooms provided feeble illumination. Cold water issued from a single tap above the brown glazed sink. Water for washing clothes and bathing had to be heated in the black iron kettle, big enough to drown a terrier, that simmered permanently on the kitchen range.

Tragedy lay in wait for the family. Before Mick, as Michael was known then, was twenty, his mother had disappeared without trace, the eldest girl had left home, the epileptic had been committed to an institution and O'Hanlon senior had died within hours of being kicked in the stomach by a horse. By then, Mick had been a cabin boy on a tramp steamer and a steward on the Mauritania. He was working as a barman at the Royal Hotel in Bangor, County Down, when he was asked by a member of the Tadler family if he would like to succeed their chauffeur, who was soon to retire.

'But your mother,' Connie protested. 'Did you never find out what happened to the poor woman?'

'It's my belief she was murdered, God rest her soul, and I told the police as much, but it did no good. She'd said once or twice that a man was following her. After seven years, she was declared missing believed dead and her file was closed. Sure, she'd be ninety or over if she was still alive.'

Compared to what O'Hanlon had been used to at home and later as a seaman, conditions at Fred's Fields, the Tadlers' manor house near Newry, were idyllic. The dry, tart smell of stale sweat and dirty underwear was nowhere to be found. His rooms above the newly-built motor house were spacious, adequately furnished and cleaned for him by one of the maids. The view across fields and woodland to the Mourne Mountains brought him time and again to his windows.

The Tadlers liked Michael, as he was henceforth known.

They enjoyed helping this personable young man with the obliging manner, the winning smile and a brow so high as to account for half his face. Country air and sustaining food gradually erased the pinched and hunted look that spoke of privation, overcrowding and primitive sanitation. Smart in his dove-grey uniform with black leather gauntlets and gaiters, he set about improving himself through correspondence courses and by unobtrusively copying the speech and manners of his employers. Long waits behind the wheel were conducive to reading and leisurely reflection. In time, he came to profit from access to the Tadlers' extensive library of unread books.

'Sure, there was no side about them, Connie. They were content to remain gentry. I found nothing but good in the Tadlers and their lovely, blossoming daughters. They rode to hounds, they entertained, they exchanged houses for maybe a month at a stretch with families like themselves, and of course they toured on the Continent in the days when French roads were often appalling and the only signposts were those provided by Rolls-Royce. I've the Tadlers to thank for everything, Connie. More wine? There's enough left for the both of us.'

'Did you ever meet members of our Royal Family?' Mrs Osborne asked.

O'Hanlon's smile broadened as he shook his head. He explained: 'The Tadlers were in trade. They earned their money and so were not received into garden party society. They owned paper mills.'

'King George and Queen Elizabeth came to Liverpool when the bombing was at its height.'

'The least they could do, Connie.'

'I'd have seen them only I'd got our Cath ill and off school and I didn't want to leave her. They drove past the end of Burnett Road after they'd been staying with Lord Derby.'

'I'm afraid I don't share your reverence for the monarchy, Connie. If I had my way, I'd sell the Royal Family to the Americans.'

'I wonder if that's because you're Irish? If you'll excuse me saying so, the Irish are a childish people. Certainly where you come from. They're squabbling and demonstrating over events that happened three hundred years ago: banging drums and setting off bombs and walking through the streets shouting "No surrender!". What's that if it isn't childish?'

'You're speaking of a noisy minority, sure, steeped in religious prejudice. The bulk of Ireland's people just want to be left in peace to get on with their lives. And I can't agree, Connie, that Irishness or childishness or prejudice have anything to do with my distaste for the monarchy.'

'Our Royal Family hold this country together, Michael. Calling them gluttonous parasites, like Dooley does, amounts to blasphemy in my view.'

'But not in mine. For me, they represent the last of the great feudal monarchies, stuffing themselves off gold plate while the rest of us bob and curtsy to them.'

'That's a very crude overstatement. The royals, as I believe they're called, do some very useful work.'

'Connie, they've never done a day's work in their lives – not work as it's understood by the rest of us. My imagination tells me that someone wakes them with their morning tea, someone draws their bath and lays out the clothes appropriate to the day's arrangements, someone puts their breakfast in front of them, someone hands them the speech they haven't written, someone tells them the car is at the door . . . D'you call that work? I wouldn't be surprised if someone goes on ahead to warm the lavatory seat for them.'

'I agree with some of the opposition to the monarchy. I've never liked our national anthem. It's dreary, selfish and antiquated.'

'E.M.Forster called it a curt series of demands upon the almighty to look after number one.'

'*Land of Hope and Glory* would be my choice. And I don't see that they need umpteen palaces and estates. One of each would be ample.'

'They're needed for the Family's numerous relatives, retainers and hangers-on. I'd give the lot of them ten years for adjustment and acclimatisation before turning them loose to provide for themselves and stand on their own feet. They could keep their titles and fancy dress, but not their free accommodation and privileges. As to the Family itself, I agree with you: if we've got to support them instead of getting rid of them completely, limit them to one town mansion and one country estate. Sell everything else, including their art treasures, and use the countless millions raised at auction to fund schools and hospitals and research into new sources of energy before the world comes to a standstill. Have you seen Buckingham Palace, St James's Palace and Kensington Palace, to name only three out of a dozen or more palatial residences, some of them standing in thousands of acres of parkland?'

'I've never set foot in London.'

'We'll go there, Connie. I'll hire a motor car and show you the sights. After the royal palaces, we'll have a look at the people sleeping in cardboard boxes, then have a tour of Brixton, Clapham and Wandsworth and see the squalor in which some of Her Majesty's subjects – I call us her benefactors – are obliged to live.'

Chapter Ten

It was late afternoon when Frank and Gloria reclaimed their suite at the Station Hotel in Wall Town at the end of a fortnight's tour of the West Country. Neither was in the best of tempers. Save for two or three calm and sunny days, the weather had been cool and wet, with wild seas and overcast skies. Frank felt frustrated by Ida Blanchard's single typewritten page, which told him little about his sister that he hadn't known already, and Gloria was annoyed at having to return to Wall Town for the meeting with Robin Blanchard that Frank had arranged by telephone.

'You're coming, aren't you?' he asked, pleasantly.

They were relaxing in their sitting room in armchairs as far apart as space would allow. Room service had brought coffee for Frank, gin and tonic for Gloria. She was biting her nails and scowling. The novelty had worn off her new car and her vision of the future was not encouraging. She cursed herself for having to have a man.

Frank repeated his question.

'No, I'm not,' she answered, sharply. 'What's more, we're leaving here tomorrow morning and we're not coming back, so don't make any further arrangements unless you want to walk home.'

'I thought maybe you'd want to meet Dorothy's husband. After all, she was your best—'

'Shut up!' cried Gloria, on the verge of tears. 'I'm sick to death of everyone and everything connected with this tomfoolery you call a biography. Throw your silly notebook in the fire and have the sense to leave writing to your betters.'

Frank was silent for a moment. Then: 'What will you do this evening?' he asked, watching Gloria rise and quickly cross the room.

'Jump off the Empire State Building,' she snapped.

She went into their bedroom and slammed the door.

A moment later, he heard her crying and guessed she was lying on her bed with her face in the pillow. She had been weepy these last two or three days and Frank surmised accurately that she was suffering women's pains.

Gloria was worried about losing her looks and becoming unattractive to men. She had never wanted children, genuine in her belief that they ruin life for sensitive people; but now that she could no longer conceive, the thought of maternity came tugging at her peace of mind, making her wonder what she had missed, even creating a sense of incompleteness. She could understand now why she invariably felt excluded and patronised by couples who had children. At however primitive a level, such people enjoyed a sense of fulfilment denied to the childless, unless the latter were creative artists, in which case intimations of immortality came from their work.

Her condition was tolerable, at any rate in its present form, provided there was a man in her life. Without one, she was as listless and forlorn as the last fly in October. Her mother had predicted that Gloria would be like a little fat pig before she was forty. That hadn't come true. Her blue eyes and delicately dressed hair, her natural teeth and floury skin, continued to make her seductive. Massage and swimming and not too much to eat had kept her figure trim enough to look its best in stiletto heels, a mini skirt and a low-cut silk blouse. She didn't need Frank Hatfield to confirm her drowsy sensuality, but she did need someone and that someone had to be male and capable of satisfying her in bed.

The thought of Frank, at first stimulating, now made Gloria sigh and shake her head. The smiling kindness and donnish humour of his unadorned personality were simply not enough for a woman who valued a powerful sexual thrust and the sort of flamboyance that Kitty admired in Charles Dooley. But who else was there? Who else would there ever be? Advancing years could leave her high and dry, with no company save that of Mavis de Lapp and the two old sticks who came up to play bridge. And when they went their way, what then? Gloria was not one to make friends easily (she didn't really care for people), so where would she find an acceptable male who wanted something more lasting than a one-night stand?

She rose from her bed and made her way to the bathroom without looking at Frank, who was listening to spoken German on the radio.

'Coffee?' he called.

'Thanks.'

'I'll ring for some fresh.'

'Tell them to bring twenty Players. I'm out of stock.'

'Why not lay off till tomorrow?' Frank asked, with a smile in his voice.

For answer, Gloria kicked the bathroom door shut with her heel.

Frank hoped she would let him kiss and comfort her. Experience of two wives helped him divine her thoughts, awakening his sympathy. Periods, pregnancies and the menopause made life difficult for all women and miserable for a minority. Men were spared not only these inconveniences, but also the pain of childbirth, which he recalled Clare saying was like no other pain. Frank agreed with her that the human reproduction mechanism was a design failure, being either the work of a simpleton or that of a woman-hater with a sadistic streak. To the burdens imposed by Nature were added those created by convention. The woman got the jobs no one else wanted. It fell to her to shop for food, to decide what to give them, and frequently to diet while cooking for a feasting family. She it was who had to remember birthdays, send Christmas cards, visit the sick, care for infirm relatives, bring up children whose father had cleared off with someone else. Small wonder that penis envy sometimes prompted women to deliberately sour the lives of their men!

Coffee and cigarettes were on the circular table between the armchairs when Gloria came out from repairing her make-up. Hearing German issuing from the radio, she crossed the room in a sudden burst of impatience and switched it off.

'You can't understand that,' she snapped, stung by this reminder of her failure to continue learning.

'I know,' Frank answered. 'That's why I'm listening to it.'

'Well, you're not listening to it now.'

'You look nice.'

Frank moved to take her in his arms.

'Leave me alone,' Gloria muttered. 'Men make me sick.'

A bone clicked in her knee as she walked to the table to pour the coffee.

'You've gone off me, haven't you?' Frank said, stripping the cellophane from the cigarette packet for her.

'I'd like you better if you didn't look and sound like a left-over from the 1930s.'

'What's wrong now?'

'Look at yourself in the glass. Here's your coffee.'

Gloria carried hers and the cigarettes to the easy chair she had occupied earlier.

'Coloured shirts and long hair are not my style, Gloria. I'm a white shirt and black shoes man.'

'You're a bore. I'd kick your arse if I thought it might produce a sign of life. When you talked the other day about becoming a councillor, I said to myself "How appropriate!". The mere word wears a cardigan and brings paste sandwiches for lunch.'

'It was just an idea for when the biography is out of the way.'

'The biography!' Gloria snorted, with voice and face full of contempt.

She blew smoke at the ceiling.

Frank said: 'I'll need an objective. Something to do. How did Raby spend his time?'

'I never found out. That's what made him new all the time.'

Sitting down and crossing one leg over the other, Frank stirred his coffee and said: 'Robin Blanchard is my last hope of getting the sort of solid material that Neen Savage the Fourth is demanding. I've got to talk with him.'

Gloria didn't respond.

'Why not come along tonight?' Frank said, coaxingly. 'You don't want to stay here on your own.'

'Who said I'm staying here on my own?'

Frank was silent.

'Where are you meeting him?' asked Gloria.

'A pub called The Tiler's Toast.'

'Where is it?'

'In a village about five miles away. Not Falling Knickers or Twitching Bottoms. Sweetwell. The locals manage to pronounce it Swettel.'

'You can make your own way. I've had all the driving I want for one day, thank you very much.'

'Come and meet him, Glorious. I don't want to go on my own. We'll have an early dinner and—'

'I've said no. I mean no. I intend to rape the pantry boy.'

But she came, at least as far as the car park. She wouldn't be persuaded out of the Morgan and into The Tiler's Toast.

'If I came face to face with your Norah Blanchard, I'd be tempted to spit in it. Robin might offer you a lift back. If he doesn't, ring me.'

'Can you see Norah sitting in a country pub, looking for all the world like Ena Sharples, hairnet an' all? I can't. Come inside, Gloria, and let me buy you a nice big Gordon's gin with tonic and lemon and tinkling ice. You're weakening. You're weakening, m'lady.'

'Listen not to the voice of the devil,' Gloria said, with a smile; and let the clutch in.

She had no intention of risking an encounter with a woman who might have known her at Rose Choir School and remembered why she was expelled from it.

2

More than a month after her meeting with Gloria and Frank, and one week after Robin's talk with Frank at The Tiler's Toast, Ida asked Robin to come to her flat for a few minutes. In that month or more, they had exchanged fewer than a hundred words and had made no mention of Frank and Gloria. Ida in her office and Robin in his kitchen worked independently of each other. He did all his own ordering while she supervised the staff and kept the accounts.

They lived separately. After leaving London together and while Bytheway House was being extended from a restaurant to a hotel, they had lived with Norah Blanchard at Arrowcross Farm. The couple with whom they had set up a partnership, Candy and Derek Comfort, had stayed at the Station Hotel in Wall Town. Once the bedroom block was built, the couples had each moved into a small flat on the premises. Identical save for the interior colour scheme, the flats were next to one another on the first floor, their windows looking out over an overgrown field at the rear of the hotel. Until the break-up of the partnership, Ida had been in charge of reception, Robin Blanchard was the chef, and Candy the housekeeper. Derek had occupied the office that was now Ida's, styling himself chairman and managing director.

The Comforts were now managing The Tiler's Toast, where Robin drank and played dominoes in such spare time as he permitted himself. Cheerful and hardworking, he had evolved into an inventive chef, often asked for his recipes by patrons of the restaurant, among whom he liked to circulate, asking in his pleasant way if the food was to their liking. This was the early 1970s, when women dressed like Gloria Raby and sombre businessmen blossomed overnight into colour-coordinated shirts, ties and suits. The convict haircut, along with the white shirt and formal tie, went into abeyance. Robin figured among those men who let their hair grow almost to shoulder length before having it set in ringlets. His hair was blond. It went with blue eyes and fair skin, a slight build and a noticeable effeminacy in voice and gesture. His bullish father, to Norah Blanchard's distress, hadn't been above telling him in company that he should have been a girl. Ida liked to taunt him with 'You little sissy. You sickly little queen', although he was not and never had been homosexual. She stopped short of mocking him in the presence of others. He knew too much about her.

Following the Comforts' departure, Robin moved into the flat they had occupied. Left to herself, Ida had one of the twin beds removed, explaining to her staff that separate accommodation was desirable because she and Robin invariably got up and came to bed at different times. She herself rarely left the hotel except to have tea with Norah or visit her hairdresser or bank manager. Robin went to The Tiler's Toast most evenings, often drinking after hours with Derek and the chosen few, then driving home well over the legal limit in his and Ida's red Riley Kestrel.

'Summoned to The Presence,' he said, without sarcasm, closing the door of Ida's flat behind him. 'What's so priceless that you couldn't tell me in my kitchen, Idaho?'

'We've got snoopers, Bobbins. Sit down and look comfortable. Shall I ring for something to drink?'

'Not for me, ducks.'

It was nine in the evening and Robin was in his unvarying off-duty outfit of grubby trainers, washed-out blue jeans and a navy tee shirt.

'I'll be off to The Tiler's after this,' he added. 'Why not come along? Give yourself a break for once.'

'And see Comfort again? No, thanks. Not after what he did to us.'

'That's all in the past. You can't go on condemning people for incompetence.'

'You don't know li'l ole Ida. Cigarette?'

'Thanks.'

'Catch.'

Ida's sitting room, like Robin's next door, could seat four people on a cream velvet sofa and twin armchairs, each with a fringed leather strap over one arm bearing a small copper ashtray. A Pembroke table, folded down now and with flowers on it, stood beneath the window, a standard lamp to one side of it, a Ferguson television to the other. The close-fitted carpet was a brown and fawn mottled tufted. Doors in one wall led to Ida's bedroom, her combined bathroom and lavatory, and a cramped kitchenette.

She came to the point.

'I had a couple here asking about Dorothy, wanting to write an article for an American magazine, I think they said. I just thought I'd warn you in case they seek you out and start making a nuisance of themselves.'

'What name?'

'Raby. From somewhere up north.'

'When was this, Idaho?'

'Oh, it's a few weeks ago. They didn't stay long. I don't think they'll come back, Bobbins, but if they do will you refer them to me?'

'Didn't they ask to see me? After all, I was Dorothy's husband.'

'I don't think they knew about you. They were only interested in Dorothy as a writer – in Mary Orchard, in other words. As her secretary, I was able to tell them all they wanted to know.'

'This is the couple you had with you in the office when I served coffee and biscuits one morning. Right?'

Ida hesitated. Then, as though suddenly remembering: 'Yes. I'd have introduced you, Bobbins, only I didn't want the meeting to run on, because you were at full stretch preparing for the Masonic half-night and I had things to do myself and quite honestly I didn't think their ideas about writing a biography would ever amount to anything. The woman was skitting at it the whole time.'

'Sure the name was Raby?'

'I think that's what she said.'

'Sure the man wasn't called Hatfield?'

'I don't think he gave his name, Bobbins. The woman did all the talking.'

'What are you frightened of, Ida?'

'Frightened? What makes you think I'm frightened?'

'The man was Dorothy's brother, which makes him my brother-in-law, and his name is Frank Hatfield.'

'He never told me that.'

'He thinks he did. He thinks he asked you to let him talk to me. I had a few pints with him at The Tiler's Toast one night last week. He was on his way north the next day to get his notes organised and begin the serious writing. It's a heavyweight biography, looking deep into Dorothy's life, and Frank rang me yesterday with the news that it'll be published in England as well as in the States.'

'What did you tell him?'

'That I'm a railway enthusiast. Full scale: twelve inches to the foot. He said women have a heart but no soul and men have a soul but no heart. He's right. Women don't appreciate old lorries and steam engines and suchlike, do they? Women live on the surface of life. Take Frank. He's into old buses, especially the Leyland Lion, but his lady thinks he's—'

'What did you tell him?'

'I mentioned the steam rally we have on Amanda Berriman's fields every July and I invited him here for it. Nice chap. We'll be talking to each other quite a lot during the writing of his book.'

'What did you tell him? Answer me!'

Robin wriggled deeper into his armchair and tilted ash off his cigarette into the copper ashtray. He was enjoying himself.

'About you?' he asked. 'About Stella?'

Ida waited, watching Robin with simmering hatred.

'Nothing,' he said.

'D'you intend telling him? You're low enough.'

'No lower than you when you spit your venom at me. Every dog has his day, Idaho. Maybe it's my turn now.'

'What d'you want?'

'What you've refused to give me ever since we came here. When we eloped from Willow Square, you said you'd play Stella once in a while. Remember?'

'Don't you think I had enough of that when I was married to Billy Prince?' Ida demanded, tensely. 'I'm not your wife, in case you've forgotten. Why should I cater for your perverted cravings?'

'Moralising isn't going to help you, old dear. I suggest you get out your black and white clothes and your high heels and brush up on the routines that once we loved so well. Just think what a spicy story it would make if I spilt your beans!'

3

Ida had come a long way since being born Ida O'Grady in a fight-a-night area of Oldham. Her father had been a brick-layer, as often in work as out of it, her mother a seamstress in the workroom of a carpet shop. No sooner had O'Grady moved his family to London in search of regular employment than he died of liver failure, leaving his wife and Ida to cope as best they could in a tenement flat in Dockside. By the time Dorothy engaged her as her secretary, Ida had been dismissed either for unpunctuality or absenteeism from a string of jobs that included cloakroom attendant, probationer nurse, bus conductress and self-taught shorthand typist of the hit or miss variety.

It was while working on the buses that she had the misfortune to meet and marry dapper little Billy Prince, a plumber by day and a song and patter man by night. He was a cockney, a teetotaler and an enthusiastic wife beater. Although she could have flattened him with one hand, Ida was frightened of him, yielding not only to his frequent need of her body but also his demand that she 'entertain' men at their home in Scrub Hill, north London. He put a postcard advertisement in a showcase outside a Soho shop, then sat in the kitchen while Ida spanked or caned the men who responded. They knew her by her advertised name of Stella and among them was Robin Blanchard.

Robin was living at the time in a basement flat in Great Homer Street, not far from the BBC, with his schoolgirl daughter, Hilary. He was between marriages. His first wife, Hilary's mother, had died beneath the wheels of a Tube train at Leicester Square Underground station, and he had still to meet Dorothy Hatfield, who was then senior nurse at a thriving West End dental practice. Marriage to lonely and spineless Robin made her mistress of his household, and a very selfish and domineering mistress she quickly showed herself to be, alienating Hilary and controlling her husband with her tongue and the flat of her hand.

She was making her way as Mary Orchard, writer of adventure stories for girls, when her agent sent Ida along in response to her need of a secretary. When Robin opened the flat door to her, recognition was immediate on both sides. So was an agreement to keep Stella secret. The marriage to dapper little Billy Prince was over, Ida was back with 'me Mam' in the Dockside tenement, and all she wanted was a new life away from men. On Robin's side, he didn't want his scolding wife to know that he enjoyed the beatings she regularly gave him.

It was Ida herself who eventually told Dorothy about Stella, at the same time explaining that throughout the ten years or so of their marriage, Robin had been finding sexual pleasure in Dorothy's mistreatment of him. Ida did so to avenge the near-fatal kicking that Dorothy gave her husband as punishment for going to Arrowcross after she had refused him permission to leave their Willow Square home. 'You crazy fool! D'you want to kill him?' Ida had shouted, having seized Dorothy from behind and dragged her away from her writhing victim. The incident, coinciding as it did with the death of Robin's father, marked the end of the marriage and of Ida's close communion with her employer.

In one of the last conversations to take place between the two women, Dorothy had steadfastly refused to believe that men, her husband included, found gratification in receiving corporal punishment from attractive women: it simply didn't make sense to her. Therefore, Stella had been offering intercourse, and the conviction that this was so made Dorothy break down in tears. 'You were nothing more than a prostitute,' she had stated; but her outrage had none of the fierceness of Ida's rebuttal. After minutes of heated accusation and denial, Dorothy had reluctantly agreed to withdraw the charge.

The fact that in her heart she remained convinced of Ida's guilt was evidenced by the new Will she made when living alone in Willow Square only weeks before her death. Earlier, when their romantic friendship was in full flower, she had told Ida to expect a considerable sum of money; but the changed Will stipulated that her house and effects were to be sold, with all proceeds going to animal charities. All Ida got were the rights to the Mary Orchard novels, which at the time appeared worthless.

And so she entered poor and penniless into the Bytheway House partnership, the necessary capital being supplied by Derek Comfort and Robin Blanchard, whose father had left him a sizeable though insignificant portion of his riches. Both men sank all they had into the enterprise.

The partners worked in harmony at first, allowing themselves scant leisure while watching with satisfaction the steadily rising turnover. Since Comfort was the only one with commercial experience, he and Candy having managed a Reklaw's pub in south London, the others left him to puff his Sherlock Holmes pipe in the office while fixing the tarifs, keeping the accounts, paying the wages and thinking of ways to improve business. By entertaining influential people, he secured the patronage of the Rotary Club, the Round Table and the Fortyone Club, all of which had previously convened at the Station Hotel.

But Candy was watching impatiently as he became ever more grandiose, noisily playing Mine Host in the bar at lunch time and in the evening, sometimes dispensing drinks, more often holding the floor while smoking a cigar and warming his buttocks at the fire. He cut an impressive figure in full hunting fig or salt and pepper trousers and dark green double breasted blazer with gilt buttons. Tall and burly, he had a deep, commanding voice, thick brown hair through which he occasionally pushed both hands, and an appetite that came close to rivalling his thirst.

In private, husband and wife bickered almost ceaselessly, with Derek usually getting the worst of it. Ida and Robin used to hear them through the wall, trading insults and slamming doors while their small son, Jamie, wailed his protest. Both had nursed artistic aspirations in the early years of their association. Living for much of the time on State benefits, Derek had made copious notes for a biographical study of Mulsanne that never got written, while Candy, in flowing robes, bare feet and blue spectacles had daubed at her easel and imagined herself graciously receiving the Jackson Pollock Award. Today, no longer twinkling bright, she was the sour-faced and sharp-tongued critic of a man whom she came eventually to accuse of mistaking his executive position for early retirement.

'While the rest of us are working ourselves silly, you're riding to hounds, shooting at Arrowcross Farm or stamping round in the snow in ski boots and an Afghan coat.'

Then there was the time Derek spent at trade fairs and business seminars, the Range Rover that replaced the elderly Triumph Stag and the dinner suit tailored in Savile Row.

'I want to make this hotel famous,' he shouted, in self-defence, 'and I'm not going to do that peeling potatoes or walking round scratching my arse in a boiler suit. Speculate to accumulate: that stands at the head of my business plan. Who brought the Masons to Bytheway House? Or the Lions Club? Who got himself interviewed at Rose Choir School and came back with a booking for their annual staff dinner?'

Ida and Robin smiled their amusement at this friend and colleague whose mix of country squire and metropolitan entrepreneur resulted in a rather endearing showman. Derek had every right, they conceded, to be intoxicated by the aroma of his success when, at the end of the partners' first accounting year, he could show a packed functions diary and an 85% average room occupancy over the twelve month period.

But the audit revealed something else. Low tarifs linked to extravagant promotional expenditure had produced a trading loss. The partners faced bankruptcy, and the embarrassed culprit, striding to an fro behind his executive desk, was reduced to shouting: 'Are you saying you've no confidence in your chairman and managing director? Is that what you're saying? Because if so, I'll leave now.'

'What else can they say?' Candy muttered, bitterly.

'We trusted you,' Robin protested, enfeebled.

Stunned, Ida murmured: 'We left it all to you.'

Norah Blanchard saved Bytheway House from closure, but on condition the partnership was dissolved and the Comforts sent packing. She it was who saw in Ida a latent business-woman and, with difficulty, made Ida see it too. Ida's initial 'What are we going to do, Bobbins? We're finished.' was replaced within days by a cool determination to succeed. Soon the woman who looked in fear at her first sales representative, imagining herself obliged to order from him, felt secure enough in her new role to have a brass plate reading MRS IDA BLANCHARD, PROPRIETRESS screwed to her office door.

Although she liked being Mrs Blanchard, just as she liked having her accountant and her solicitor, she insisted on her staff calling her Ida. She was good to them, ever mindful that a good mistress is sometimes blind and a good servant sometimes deaf, but she was firm as well. By the time Frank and Gloria met her, Bytheway House was solvent and making money, the unexpected sale of Dorothy's rights to Hamilton Jupp Incorporated having cleared Norah's generous loan with cash enough left over for repairs and renovations.

People liked Ida. Once it became known that on Mondays and Fridays she stationed herself in the bar between 6 and 7pm, locals dropped in to swell the hotel guests, and they came not for the free cocktails that were offered but to chat with Ida, to wait for the slow smile that lifted her chin slightly and to hear her sore throat voice. There was no pretence about her, no attempt to modify her north Manchester accent and intonation. What shone from her famous green eyes was the integrity and good humour that had recently prompted Norah, supported by the Master of the exclusive West Property Hunt, to propose her for the next vacancy on the local Bench.

Alone in her flat after Robin had left for The Tiler's Toast, she stared sightlessly at the certainty of losing everything if her past as Stella became known. Although it sickened her, making her loathe men for the demands they made on women, she would have to resume the role or risk Robin's telling Frank Hatfield all he knew about her life with dapper little Billy Prince.

Chapter Eleven

Connie Osborne's motoring holiday with Michael O'Hanlon grew from one week to three and she returned from it with a marriage proposal. It was her third, the first of them dating back to the late 1920s, when she was a comely brunette with dull hazel eyes, a calm acceptance of life and the incurable cough that had pestered her since infancy. She was numerate and literate, being a natural reader, mostly of Victorian fiction, and quick enough with figures to be liberated quite early from menial work.

At the time of that first proposal, Connie was employed as a cashier at Liverpool's biggest department store, using Exchange Station to travel to and from the family home in Fox Hill, sometimes buying flowers to take to her mother from the flower shop in the station concourse, never thinking that one day, when a middle-aged widow, she would rent and run it herself.

Like everyone else on the payroll, she worked long hours at the department store, which stayed open till 7pm Monday to Friday, 9pm on Saturday. In the interests of promoting diligence and maintaining discipline, the management sacked two sales assistants every week. From the elevated cash office in the middle of the basement sales floor, Connie regularly saw women and girls in tears behind their counters following abuse from a customer or a cutting reprimand from one of the hated floorwalkers. The shop assistant in the interwar years was the easy victim of the henpecked husband and the unloved wife. A complaint of slow or indifferent service could and did furnish the management with the excuse it needed for one of the ritual Saturday night sackings. There were at least twenty applicants for every vacancy, resulting in low wages and no entitlement to overtime payment before 7pm. Assistants were not allowed to sit down. Standing behind their counters, without tea breaks and with only half an hour's fresh air in the middle of the day, women and girls sometimes fainted from exhaustion.

'We never want those days back, do we, Connie?' O'Hanlon remarked, when once again the couple were sharing wine and sandwiches in the living room at Burnett Road. 'Why, I've seen dockers fight each other with their bare fists when the checker at Belfast docks came out and told a bunch of them waiting outside the gates that there was a day's work for three or maybe four out of a dozen or more. But you were going to tell me about your fine young man, Leslie Montgomery.'

The Irishman sat forward in his fireside chair, a broadening grin beneath a prominent nose seeming to split his face in halves as Mrs Osborne began to describe the bank employee whom she had met coming out of church and later at a whist drive and whose desire to marry her had evaporated on learning that he would lose his job if he did.

'I thought t'was only women who were obliged to leave off work when they married,' O'Hanlon observed. 'That was the way of it in Ireland, sure.'

'It was the same over here. If a married woman went out to work before the Second World War, she did it on the sly, because it meant her husband couldn't support her and that was considered shameful. She had more than enough to do in the home anyway, what with brushing and scrubbing on her hands and knees and coping with a mountain of washing and ironing. Because there were no refrigerators, she had to shop for food every day. The nearest ordinary people got to a fridge was a meat safe outside the kitchen door.'

Leslie Montgomery was the accountant at Martineau's bank in the Liverpool district of Ferndown. Females were rarely employed in the banking world of the 1920s and '30s, and then only as behind-the-scenes typists or clerkesses. The tellers, as Martineau's called their cashiers, were mature men drawn from Mariner's or Liverpool College who stood at intervals behind an unguarded counter of polished wood, each with his ready-reckoner out of sight and a set of brass scales at his side for weighing shillings and pence, florins and half-crowns. They looked, spoke and dressed like gentlemen. Dark suits with waistcoats were obligatory all week, but sports clothes were permitted on Saturday morning so that the tellers could go straight to some leisure activity when the branch closed at 12.30.

Connie said: 'I wasn't being truthful when I said Monty would lose his job if he went ahead and married me. Better to say he'd have ruined his chances of promotion.'

He was over twenty-five when the couple became engaged and so didn't need his manager's permission to marry. But the Martineau family had him in mind for management, which brought with it occupancy at a nominal rent of the flat above the branch. This was considered an important position, combining responsibility with a certain amount of entertaining, and it was for the family to decide whether Connie would make a suitable wife for Leslie Montgomery, as tall and handsome as he was charming and ambitious.

Connie was requested to attend for interview at the company's main branch in Castle Street. Behind the desk sat young Roger Martineau, whose interest in female legs made girls blush and women glare at his shameless eyes while tugging at their skirts.

'I'd never been inside a bank before. Neither had Mum and Dad. Only employers and monthly paid staff had cheque books. If you wanted an account, you had to be recommended by a customer before the manager weighed you up and said yes or no.'

Banking, drinking and schooling were among the activities that took place behind high window sills and opaque glass. True to type, Martineau's in Castle Street was a white stone fortress with black steel street doors, marble floors, polished mahogany counters backed by matching partitions, and softly revolving fans in the vaulted ceiling.

Connie was coldly received in the banking hall by one of two bank messengers, remote and supercilious in pink cutaways, who stood at lecterns placed several feet from each other. He motioned her without a word to a bench, where she waited for several minutes, staring rigidly ahead in her imitation leopard skin coat and white winkle-picker shoes, her hair taken up for the occasion and encircled like a girdle cake with a band of ice blue satin. Eyes, lips and cheeks were heavily made up.

'I was out of my depth,' she could admit, more than forty years later. 'They were expecting a girl from Swandella or Notre Dame, not one who'd left school at fourteen and gone to work in a laundry.'

She had been awed into petrified silence by Roger Martineau, urbane and immaculate in black jacket and striped trousers, with white slips to his waistcoat and a gold ring beneath the half-Windsor of his Salopian tie. When it came her turn to speak, she jumped up and fled without a word.

'But didn't Monty tell you what to expect?' O'Hanlon asked.

'Not a word. He knew, but he didn't want me to know. Monty knew I wouldn't be approved - a tongue-tied girl of eighteen - and that would provide him with an excuse for breaking off our engagement. He was tired of me. He'd been amusing himself - that's all.'

But not quite. Like many another courting couple in those days, their walks had ended with breathless love-making in the park.

'Did you sue for breach of promise, Connie?'

Offended, Mrs Osborne retorted: 'Certainly not!'

Jilted girls who sued were held in low esteem.

She continued: 'We should never have contemplated marriage. My mother told me from the start that I wasn't his class. His sister didn't have to. She just took her sewing into the next room. I gave him his ring back - foolishly, perhaps. He didn't ask for it and I know how much it cost.'

'What were your feelings, Connie?'

'I was flattered when he seemed to want me. I couldn't stop looking at my engagement ring; turning it this way and that to catch the light and wanting everyone to notice it. I was fond of him. I'll always remember the little dance he used to do for me. I didn't bother looking for someone else for months. I spent a whole winter reading Anthony Trollope's novels, one after the other, loving every sentence. Have you ever been in love, Michael?'

'Only with my liberty. My freedom, sure. I never needed a family; for I had warmth all around me. That's what I miss today: companionship. I had the servants' hall an' all and the Tadlers too. How did you meet Harry Osborne, Connie? He didn't come in a Christmas cracker.'

'His trousers came down the moment he saw me.'

'Begin the way you intend to carry on. That was his motto, Connie.'

Harry Osborne was an engineer with the Bell Line, whose chief source of revenue was the importation of bananas. Unusually for a seafarer, he kept to himself, drank little and never went roistering ashore. He spent his off-watches resting in his cabin, sitting out on deck or playing chess with Bob Stilt, the radio officer. Fear of venereal disease kept him chaste until his marriage to Connie.

It was Bob Stilt who brought them together. The place was the Tower Ballroom in New Brighton, the time New Year's Eve 1929. Connie was there with her then unmarried sister, Flo, who had been asked to dance by Stilt, Connie having already got up to partner someone else. When the sisters came together again, Stilt invited them to join him and his friend at their table on the balcony.

'Harry stood up to be introduced and that's when his trousers hit his shoes,' Connie explained. 'He'd forgotten he'd unfastened them under the table to take the pressure off his hernia.'

He was short and thickset, his square face enhanced by keen eyes and teeth that were as white as they were rock solid. Even in children, such teeth were rare before the advent in 1948 of the National Health Service. A mouth disfigured by missing or rotten teeth was commonplace within the lower class, where meagre wages and uncertain employment put dental care out of reach. False teeth, made of porcelain and set in mica, were expensive, uncomfortable, and as uniform as railings.

'Harry came ashore for his hernia operation and a period of calm, and we were married before he went back to sea,' Connie remembered. 'He had medical insurance, so didn't have to go cap in hand to the Lady Almoner to ask for charity. I'm told every hospital had a Lady Almoner and some of them treated poor people as if they smelt.'

'There were plenty who did, Connie, in the courts and tenements of Belfast. Children in rags, children with no shoes or socks, children with dirty hands and faces and crying because their bellies were empty. Sure, I'll never forget the smell of poverty as long as I live.'

When 'poor dear Donald' was born in 1930, Harry Osborne, firm in his belief that a married man's place was with his family, left the Bell Line to join the engine room staff of Wallasey Ferries, where he remained until his death. His strong sense of duty kept him solvent and ever mindful of the welfare of his wife and their children.

Connie said: 'I never got close to him, never really knew what he was thinking. Fortunately, I loved reading, so his long silences, sucking on his pipe behind the *Echo*, meant I could read my library book without feeling I ought to be making conversation.'

'Did you love him, my dear?'

'I respected him. He never hurt my feelings and he was good to the children, buying them little presents and taking them out for the day. Harry was all right. I was a dependable wife and mother, I made a comfortable home for him, but I did sometimes look at the back page of his *Echo* and wonder if he wished he'd stayed at sea. I've always considered sea-going a nice life for a man. If Harry had stayed deep sea, he'd probably have been a chief engineer by the time he retired.'

'He was a far-seeing man, Connie. He married because, being wiser than me, he saw early on the need of an anchorage for his old age. He was a practical man, whose head ruled his heart, much as Monty's had done, and he didn't come ashore till he was satisfied he'd found the right one.'

Like Charles Dooley, Osborne had been a purely physical man who saw not the lily and the rose. Aside from his work and a meticulous combing of the morning and evening papers, his only interest was an increasing one in the pigeons housed at the bottom of the garden. As 'my birds' slowly pushed Connie into the background, Osborne took to sitting with them for perhaps an hour at a time, finding serenity in their soft cooing, which Connie called burping and heartily disliked.

'He was maybe trying to understand their language, Connie,' O'Hanlon suggested, beaming with good humour as he shared the last of the wine with her. 'Are you one of those people who believe language is exclusive to humans? Not me. If you ask me, humans have invented nothing that doesn't already exist in Nature. We've taken what we found and refined it, that's all. What's a flea, Connie, if it isn't a heat-seeking missile? What are telecommunications if not the Central Nervous System? What's a computer if it isn't a pale imitation of the human brain? What an amount we've learned from the so-called lower animals! Lower? Who gets lower than Man when it comes to greed, hypocrisy and cruelty? Pascal called Man the glory and the excrement of the universe and Pascal was right.'

'You don't think it's going to last much longer, do you, Michael? And I think I agree with you.'

'The world, you mean? How can it when we're raping, plundering and polluting it at an ever-increasing speed? Consider the millions of tons of buried household and industrial waste that is putrifying and leaching in landfill sites! Consider rising temperatures and their effect on our weather and the world's water levels! The end of the oil supply will cripple us and pollution will poison us. It's only a matter of time.'

'Perhaps it's just as well we're old, Michael.'

'Well, put it this way, Connie. I wouldn't be Cathy or Charles for anything – still less little Miranda.'

2

O'Hanlon was always welcome at 4, Burnett Road. His affability and good manners were inborn, his tact and erudition acquired during his many years in service to the 'lovely family', to which he frequently referred. He had chauffeured them all over Europe and now, happy in his retirement, he found himself being chauffeured by Charles Dooley.

'You come with me any time you like, old sport. Just say the word. Okay?' Dooley said, when they were driving from Liverpool to Ketter's Nottingham store. 'I've got us rooms at the Savoy, where the steak's good and the beer even better.'

His voice normally had the light, whining quality that provided Mrs Osborne with one of her reasons for disliking him, but it mellowed to a boisterous heartiness when the company was exclusively male. He could be himself with men. They were synonymous with foaming pints, coarse jokes, loud laughter and talk of cars and football. With women, on the other hand, he felt he had to be on his best behaviour, anointing them with the warm oils of his flattery and retaining their favour with little courtesies, small presents and a nervous flow of light conversation. Had you told him he was frightened of women, you would have touched a nerve that was all the more tender for being deeply buried. Dooley didn't know why they scared him and he resented the fact that they did, seeing it as a slur on his masculinity.

He very much wanted to be friends with Connie, as we usually do with those who are distant or changeable with us, but she continued to find words and silences designed to hurt him, although he was smart enough to cover the wound with banter. There was a streak of nastiness in her character and now and then she needed someone upon whom to exercise it. Kitty had been an easy target when living at home and in unhappy bondage to Clive Rolls. But her natural gaiety and resilience made her less vulnerable than her mother would have preferred, and now that she had her man and her baby she was virtually unassailable. 'Who's going to look at you, for pity's sake?' Connie might snort, lowering her library book to view Kitty making herself extra attractive before going out on Saturday night. 'No one'll even notice you.' But Dooley was at hand to gently remove the dart with a well-turned and sincere compliment for his queen.

He wondered now, on leaving his car and walking towards Ketter's with O'Hanlon, how the Irishman would find Connie as a permanent companion. She was moulting slowly into brighter plumage, releasing a little of herself at a time so as not to let anyone think she was enjoying her situation. Sure enough, when Kitty teased her about the forthcoming event, gleefully calling her Connie O'Hanlon, she responded with good humour; but the essential woman remained unchanged, the woman who had known how to send Harry Osborne off to work feeling wretched. Dooley suspected that she would find a way of turning the 'lovely family' round on Michael.

'Have you decided where you're going to live, Mike?' he asked.

'We've been to see the block of retirement flats they're putting up along the road from where Cathy used to teach dancing. We'll likely settle for one of those.'

'Well, as I've told you, you're both welcome to live with Kit and I for as long as it takes to find the right place. Don't think you've got to take the first that comes along.'

'Thank you, Charles.'

'Here's the lift. After you.'

'Where are we going?'

'Third floor. Yours Truly is about to introduce you to Maurice Zerdin. Decent bloke. Very boarding school. Dependable as the morning fart, which is why I give his company all my flooring work.'

The lift doors opened to reveal a third floor emptied of fixtures and fittings to allow floorlayers to cover the entire surface with new carpet tiles.

'I normally specify Barry's linoleum, the heavy stuff, but this time I'm trying something new,' Dooley explained, as Maurice Zerdin, lofty and casual in elderly blazer and cavalry twill, strolled towards the new arrivals with a wan smile on his long and rather sad face.

Dooley immediately became loud, breezy, and almost mocking in his familiarity. He liked Maurice, but not as much as he liked the power he had over him. Mistakenly introducing O'Hanlon as his future brother-in-law, he went on to call Maurice 'me ole son' and to ask after Helen and 'the kids'.

'How did I know you was here before us?' he thundered, as they began an inspection of the work in hand.

'You saw the Vulcan parked in the loading bay,' Maurice answered.

Dooley guffawed.

'Right! I've just got to take Mike here to look at the Vulcan before we leave,' Dooley said. 'Mike, it was the first motor lorry Zerdin's ever bought - about 1925, I shouldn't wonder - and it's an old charmer. Everything made of wood, beautifully painted, and maintained like you see in museums. Eh, Maurice? I'll tell you what, Mike: Maurice likes it so much he won't let nobody else drive it.'

'Crash box, Mr Zerdin?' O'Hanlon surmised, wistfully.

'Oh yes. No synchromesh gears when the Vulcan was built,' Maurice confirmed. 'The only thing that isn't authentic is the cushion I've allowed myself on the wooden bench seat. The man my father engaged to drive it must have had a cast iron posterior, because she's tightly sprung and most of Liverpool's streets in his time were paved with setts to provide grip for horses.'

Little save personnel had changed at Zerdin's in the near fifty years since the Vulcan, impeccably liveried in navy, gold and white, had taken to the road for the first time. Floor preparation and finishes, adhesives and laying techniques were unaltered, but not so the attitude of the men who worked on their hands and knees. The imposition of Selective Employment Tax in the 1960s had had a consequence unforeseen by politicians with little experience of life and still less of business. To avoid paying it, numerous employers sacked their hourly-paid workers and immediately re-engaged them as self-employed, Zerdin's being no exception. Former payroll employees thus became subcontractors, working not just for Zerdin's but for rival flooring contractors as well. By working long hours and wherever they were needed, they could make enough money to transform their lifestyle. The handcart and the billycan vanished, and with them the bib-and-brace culture exemplified by the workman who stood around, a Woodbine concealed in his hand, waiting for the boss to tell him what to do. The same man, now working for himself, had his own transport, a telephone at home, a bank account, freedom to work when and where he chose, and a totally new attitude to the men who hired him.

And Dooley didn't like it. His reaction paralleled the bitter indignation felt by well-to-do patrons of concert hall and opera house when the gramophone made the world's finest music available to common people. Dooley assumed equality with Helen and Maurice Zerdin, even though he suspected they despised him in secret for the ruffian he knew himself to be, but a similar assumption on the part of liberated floorlayers both angered and flustered him. He referred to them disparagingly as hunkies and he wanted them kept down. Instead, in every trade that came within his orbit, they were catching up, even outstripping him: taking the car abroad, staying in hotels instead of holiday camps, calling him Charles instead of Mr Dooley, and everywhere showing a self-confidence born of independence and rising prosperity.

'Some of them are taking home a thousand pounds a week,' Maurice said, with a wry smile; adding, when Dooley showed his scandalised astonishment: 'It's rare and they have to work night and day and sleep in the van, but it happens. Times are changing, Charles. We've just engaged our first woman floorlayer.'

'You're joking! What? Heaving heavy rolls of lino off lorries and up flights of stairs?'

'Oh yes. She has to adjust to the work, not the other way round.'

'Hear that, Mike?' Dooley cried, as one stricken. 'Jesus Christ! They'll be growing beards and using men's toilets next.'

He saw danger ahead if the female invasion of the labour market continued to spread and intensify.

'Us blokes'll be left with just the heaving and pushing if we don't watch out,' he declared. 'I can see this leading to trouble at home and violence towards women. Can't you, Mike? How would you feel if you was working in a hole in the ground while your missis was swanning round in a company car? None too chuffed is the answer.'

O'Hanlon said: 'I'd feel even worse, sure, if I was wearing a pinny and rubber gloves. I wouldn't take kindly to the little woman coming home and demanding to know what I'd been doing all day while she was out earning the money. What say you to that, Charles?'

'I say it's time for a pot of beer. Coming, Maurice? I need a gallon after what you've just told me.'

For the rest of the day and at intervals thereafter, Charles was prey to the sweat-raising vision of a society dominated by women.

3

In the course of their journeys together, Dooley became a tickled listener to Michael's adventures as a chauffeur, likewise to his observations on a variety of subjects. Not being a reader, he never ceased to be amazed that Michael could talk about events that took place before he was born.

'Am not a-kiddin' of you, I love this geezer,' he told Mrs Osborne and Kitty over a Sunday evening game of Newmarket. Wagging his head in mirthful incredulity, he slapped Michael on the back. 'He teaches me samfink ev'ry day. Who ever heard of the New Model Army or the Boston Tea Party?'

'I'm sure Connie has,' Michael said, smiling at her.

'Or cuckoos,' declared Dooley. 'That's another thing. Did you know the cuckoo is fostered? That when he's fledged, he flies from England to Egypt to join a mavver and farver he's never even seen?'

'More wine anybody?' Kitty asked.

'He flies alone and always at night. Am I right, Michael?' said Connie.

''Tis so and 'tis a miracle, sure. His brain's no bigger than a pinhead, yet it contains in miniature the flight deck of a Boeing 707. How he knows where to go and how to get there – in the dark, as Connie's just said – is as big a mystery as the Great Pyramid at Gizeh, with its blocks of stone weighing sixteen tons each and bonded together with cement of tissue paper thickness. No mortal man built that pyramid, unless he was privy to knowledge that's since been lost or destroyed, through carelessness perhaps or by jealous holy men: knowledge of levitation especially and of lasers for cutting and alignment. I've often thought, by the way, how wonderful t'would be if knowledge was transmitted from parents to children. If it was, you could say we were evolving a superman – driving towards God instead of away from him – and this would give a clear and worthwhile purpose to life.'

'Oh eh! Am gunna name a planet after you, Mike,' Dooley promised.

'Where would we put all that knowledge?' asked Kitty. 'Our brains would burst.'

'Better to live and learn, then die and forget it all. Eh, Kit?' said Dooley.

Connie recalled having read somewhere that the Great Pyramid had been built by men from outer space as a landmark for their craft.

O'Hanlon said: ''Tis what I believe, sure. It fits the legend that the twelve gods used to visit Earth from Olympus until they tired of the ways of men and stopped coming.'

'Mike's full of ideas, some of them nutty, but I like what he said to me in Nottingham about weddings and funerals,' Dooley stated. He gave his sizzling chortle before continuing with: 'He said – what was it, Mike? – a good funeral is worth a year's weddings put together: a couple of stiff whiskies, a good feed and the rest of the day to yourself. No speeches, no obligation to look cheerful and no having to spend any money. What was the last bit, old son?'

O'Hanlon glanced anxiously at the women.

'I don't think we should be discussing weddings and funerals in the same breath, Charles,' he cautioned. 'Not in view of coming events.'

Lighting a cigarette, Kitty looked briefly at Connie and Michael and wondered how their marriage would work out. Both claimed they sought companionship, but Kitty feared O'Hanlon might be expecting more of it than Connie was willing to give. When declining health had obliged her to give up the flower shop in Exchange Station, she had told Kitty that she might have to take in a lodger, adding that she wouldn't mind having one in the house if she could be sure she would never see or hear him. In so saying, she had revealed not only the possibility of needing money, but also an important aspect of her character. Her daughter's aside, Mrs Osborne didn't welcome company except at moments of her own choosing. She had no more patience with chit-chat than she had taste for 'the rubbish that gets on television'. Connie was a woman who needed frequent retreats into solitude, a solitude in which to 'gather myself together' and be miserable in peace.

'Don't ask me why I've accepted Michael,' she had already cautioned Kitty, lest optimism take root. 'It wouldn't bother me if I never set eyes on him again.'

This brought the desired reaction.

'Oh, Mother! Honestly, you're hopeless! This time yesterday you were saying how nice it'll be to have someone to talk to who's got a bit of nous about him and how much you enjoyed Wednesday night at the British Legion. What's gone wrong all of a sudden?'

'Nothing really. I'll be all right.'

'Your trouble is you won't let yourself be happy. Relax, Connie O'Hanlon! Let each wave wash you a little further up the shore.'

Mrs Osborne sniffed and looked into the fire.

'Perhaps he'll go away with Dooley from time to time,' she said, baiting the hook a second time.

'Well, for heaven's sake! Don't say that to the poor man or he'll wonder what he's taking on. Look on the sunny side: that's what I always say. You'll have a lovely new flat to furnish any way you like, you'll have evenings at the Playhouse, motor trips to London and all over. Mike's a treasure and you're a very lucky woman, if you ask me.'

A double wedding had been arranged at the register office, the couples being each other's witnesses before going by taxi to Orquinn's for a celebratory luncheon. Afterwards, Michael and Connie would stay at Burnett Road to look after Miranda while her parents enjoyed a honeymoon before Kitty began to show.

'Have you made up your minds where you're going yet, Cathy?' O'Hanlon asked, when the game of Newmarket was over and Connie had gone into the kitchen to prepare supper.

'Not yet,' Dooley answered, before his queen could reply that a honeymoon destination is supposed to be secret.

He had returned from Nottingham in a bullish frame of mind, asserting his authority by telling Kitty to contact the register office and change the date she had fixed for a later one of his choosing. He claimed to have overlooked an annual store survey that clashed with her choice and must take precedence.

For the honeymoon, the couple had considered a cruise to Mediterranean ports, a railway holiday in India, and a visit to Royal Ascot, where Charles could be bluff and peremptory in hired finery, with Kitty bewitching in a Dolly Varden hat and lemon yellow muslin. In the end, neither of them being at heart adventurous, they settled on a motoring holiday in the West Country and invited Michael O'Hanlon to choose where they would spend their first night away from home.

After supper, when the dishes had been cleared away, Dooley fetched his road atlas and gazetteer from the Morris and sat O'Hanlon down at the table with a pin in his right hand, the atlas open in front of him, and instructions to close his eyes and stab.

'Wall Town,' he announced, on opening them.

'Has a Roman sound,' mused Mrs Osborne, from her wing chair. She sniffed. 'Have you heard of it, Charles? You're our Baedeker.'

Dooley hadn't. Connie guessed accurately that he hadn't heard of Baedeker either.

'Not big enough to support a Ketter's department store,' he observed, consulting the gazetteer. 'Population 2658. Andover 17 miles. Salisbury 11. Early closing Wednesday.'

'Magic lantern in Parish Hall once a week. Barber in attendance first Monday in the month,' suggested Michael.

'Hampshire isn't exactly the West Country, but it'll do for one night,' Dooley decided. 'Or am I reading this wrong? Is Wall Town in Wiltshire? Does it matter?'

Kitty said: 'Let me look, Chummy. How many hotels are there and how many stars have they got?'

'Half a one between them,' Michael said.

Kitty found that Wall Town had two hotels.

'And neever of 'em called the New Leaf, I trust,' Charles thundered, delightedly. 'Cor, that boring bloke! That relic of the Bronze Age!'

Then he remembered Connie.

'If you're referring to Frank Hatfield,' she said, sharply, 'I can only say there are many things in his nature that others might do well to copy. Frank Hatfield is a gentleman.'

'Let's not talk about Frank, Mother,' Kitty said, quietly. 'He's gone completely out of my life.'

'It wasn't me who mentioned him,' Mrs Osborne pointed out.

'The Station Hotel and Bytheway House Hotel,' Kitty read aloud from the gazetteer. 'Bytheway House, by the way, is dearer.'

O'Hanlon remarked that station hotels are usually old, with noisy plumbing, creaking floorboards and no parking.

'The Tadlers wouldn't stay in a railway hotel,' he recalled.

Dooley said: 'Try Bytheway House, Kit. In the morning. Tell them to send us a brochure and a tarif.'

'Someone's off to bed,' Kitty told him under her breath. Aloud, she said: 'You're not going up yet, surely, Mother?'

'Can't I go to bed when I like now?' Mrs Osborne countered.

She bade a formal goodnight to O'Hanlon, who got to his feet to look at her in surprise, and then grimly made for the door.

'Is your mother all right, Cathy?' he asked, anxiously, when she had left the room.

'She's just tired, Mike, that's all,' Kitty replied.

'Sure, I know that feeling.'

'I'll see you in the morning,' Mrs Osborne announced, returning briefly to address the party from the doorway, a glass of water in her hand and a folded newspaper under her arm.

O'Hanlon, still standing, wished her a second goodnight, no less baffled than the first.

'Like me to come up with you, Mum?' Kitty asked, wanting O'Hanlon to believe that her mother wasn't too well. 'Sure you're all right?'

'Perfectly all right, thank you. I'll close this door.'

'Sleep well, Connie,' Charles sang out, feigning absorption in the road atlas. 'And God bless, eh?'

After the door had closed, the survivors stood looking in silence at it until Dooley broke the spell with: 'As my boss would say, polishing his glasses on his tie "Charles! Consider yourself crushed".'

Chapter Twelve

In the bedroom of her flat at Bytheway House Hotel, Ida was changing into the clothes that Robin Blanchard obliged her to wear when playing the part of Stella. He would be with her shortly to enjoy his now weekly dose of humiliation and corporal punishment. To date, since requiring her to meet his demands, she had spanked him over her knee, slapped and spat in his face, and knocked him about while he was dressed in female underwear. This evening she was to cane him, and in the coming week she would have to enter the hotel kitchen and scold him in front of the waitresses. If she refused, he would tell Frank Hatfield everything he knew about her years with dapper little Billy Prince, who had sat in the kitchen of their north London home while she 'entertained' men in the next room, and its publication would mean the end of everything she had worked for.

Lying awake at night, hating every second of what she had to do to ensure Robin's silence, Ida considered killing him. She wished now that she hadn't circumvented the possibility of his dying only a few days earlier, when two men had brought him home drunk and incapable from The Tiler's Toast and laid him on his bed in the flat he occupied next to hers. Before leaving, one of them had propped Robin on his side with pillows and cushions, explaining to Ida that if he lay on his back he could swallow his tongue or choke on his vomit. After they'd gone, Ida had gently removed the supports, leaving Robin snoring open-mouthed on his back. She had undressed and gone to bed, where she listened to his raucous breathing on the other side of the wall and waited with bated breath for it to stop abruptly. But before that happened, her conscience made her return to his bedside and restore him to the position in which the men had left him.

Frank's biography obsessed her, quickening her heartbeat, shortening her temper and making her neglect her work to scour the book pages of the quality newspapers for news of its publication. Dorothy Blanchard used to 'knock off' a full length Mary Orchard novel in six weeks, often laughing with pleasure at the speed with which she could dictate a coherent and readable tale. Knowing no better, Ida presumed that all books were written with similar rapidity. Where then was the biography?

'Six weeks!' echoed Anthony Quinnis, with whom she had talked in the bar before coming upstairs to change her clothes. 'Six years, more like it! I need twelve months to write one of my Two Smart Men novels and they're only light fiction.'

'Could we sit down for a moment, Mr Quinnis?'

'Are you all right, Mrs Blanchard? It is rather hot in here.'

'I'll be fine in a moment. Tell me, how's your book-signing coming along? Do the good citizens of Wall Town buy your novels?'

'We sold five copies today, eight yesterday. I've no complaints. Leslie Charteris will be at the shop next week to promote his new Saint book.'

'He's staying here. Why should a life story take so long to write, Mr Quinnis?'

'It's the research, Mrs Blanchard, as much as the writing. A good biographer digs deep into the life and times of his subject, collecting photographs and letters and people's recollections. He leaves no stone unturned.'

Six years! Six years of suspense, six years of pandering to Robin's perversion, six years before she would know if he had told Frank Hatfield about Stella. In her flat, dressed now in the white blouse and short black skirt, black nylons and black patent leather court shoes that Robin demanded, Ida walked fretfully up and down, into and out of her bedroom, twisting together hands that were damp with sweat. Close to tears, she sank into a chair beside her telephone and found the number in Redstone Bay that Frank had left with her.

As she reached for the receiver, the telephone rang, making her jump and catch her breath. The caller, put through by the hotel receptionist, was a delighted Norah Blanchard.

'Ida, dear! Such lovely news! You're a Justice of the Peace. I got the glad tidings from Sir William not ten minutes ago. Congratulations and welcome to the Bench! I'm so pleased for you, my dear.'

Ida said, huskily: 'Thank you, Norah. Thank you.'

'My joy and my pleasure. I've said it before, Ida, and I'll say it just once more. I wish you were my daughter.'

'Thank you. I'll see you tomorrow as usual.'

Would Norah want Stella for her daughter? It was essential that Ida befriend Frank Hatfield, that she try to get him on her side. But Robin mustn't know of their meeting. She had only time to say this to Frank and to ask him to ring back next day before she heard Robin leaving his flat. She replaced the receiver as he entered hers.

'We had a busy restaurant,' he began, slipping out of his white chef's jacket and throwing it on the sofa. 'They all came at once. You look cross, Idaho. Does that mean you're in the right mood for chastising naughty boys?'

'You'll find out when I start on you,' Ida said, ominously.

She stood up, watching him with smouldering hatred, and began the ritual devised at Scrub Hill, north London, and adapted for a hotel with thin walls and people passing along corridors. The possibility that members of staff might be listening added to her inner tension, making her manner as imperious as Robin or any of her former clients could have desired.

She made him fetch her cane, then her mattress, which she told him to stand on its end against the door before rolling an armchair up to it to keep it from falling.

'Now come here,' she said, holding the cane level across her thighs. 'Kneel on the floor in front of me.'

She ordered him to kiss her shoes, then the hem of her skirt, then her cane.

'I'm going to make you bend over. Then I'll give you six cuts for disobedience. Prepare yourself.'

Robin started begging for mercy, stroking Ida's legs from the ankles over the backs of the knees and upwards.

'Don't you dare put your hands up my skirt!' she snapped. 'For that, I'll cane you all the harder. Get up!'

'No, no, no! Please don't beat me, Miss Ida, please! I promise never to disobey you again.'

'Get up! Do as you're told this minute, before I lose my temper with you.'

Robin scrambled to his feet, still pleading with Ida to let him off the punishment. She ordered him to an armchair, tapping its back with her cane, and made him kneel on the seat and bend over the back.

'Now you'll get it,' she said, through clenched teeth. 'Keep still. D'you hear? If you dare move, I'll whip you till you scream.'

Bracing herself with her feet as far apart as her skirt would allow, Ida set about her victim.

One. Pause. Two. Pause. Three.

'Easy on!' Robin gasped, squirming under the unusual severity of the beating.

'Shut up!' Ida commanded. 'One more word and I'll make you drop your trousers and your underpants.'

Robin hissed and writhed as Ida administered the last three cuts.

'Boy, you meant that, didn't you?' he complained, gingerly getting down from the armchair. 'Someone skip out without paying?'

'You wanted the cane. I gave you the cane,' Ida replied, curtly. 'Put the mattress back where it belongs and get out.'

Contemptuously, she threw the cane into a corner and lit a cigarette. When alone, she would console herself with a powerful whisky and water.

Robin came out of the bedroom gently rubbing his buttocks.

'I'll settle for the hairbrush next time,' he decided, ruefully.

Ida, sick with disgust, kept her back turned until he hit the floor.

2

Ida imagined that the biographer and his lady would rally to her call as traders to the Lutine Bell at Lloyd's, which is struck once for bad news and twice for good. They didn't. As day followed day without a return call, her fear grew that they were already using material obtained from Robin to write something harmful about her. Mounting anxiety drove her at last to ring Osprey Court again.

'That female fancies you,' Gloria muttered, after Frank had replaced the receiver. 'I saw it the moment she set eyes on you.'

She was smoking and reading the *Merseyside Express* on the sofa that faced the copperbound gas fire in her drawing room.

'Attraction is usually mutual,' Frank answered, taking up Gloria's binoculars to scan the horizon. 'She wants to see me about the biography.'

'The biography!' Gloria scoffed, irritably rattling the newspaper. 'If I weren't so inhibited, I'd spit on the floor and make you clean it up. I'm not going back there.'

'You're not invited.'

'Thanks.'

'The secrecy baffles me, simple country boy that I am. When Ida rang the first time, we were to meet her at the Station Hotel. All very cloak and dagger. Now she says to come to Bytheway House.'

'I hope she debags you.'

'She has a husband.'

'I've never known that stop a determined woman. She's invited you to stay the night, I assume?'

'I could hardly do the round trip in a day.'

'Have a nice time, dearie. She'll give you one so long as you don't turn up in your Chester Barrie suit, carrying a German grammar and explaining that for the fishes in the brook, nuzzling the current, the world hasn't changed in one iota since the beginning of time. I'm sure the two old sticks from downstairs were enthralled when you told us that last night. And remember that Green Eyes may not share your ear fetish. What was it again? Why are human ears sculpted when those of cats and dogs are not? Oh, mister! – there's no one like you to set a girl ablaze with celestial fire.'

'You're keeping notes. Copycat!'

No answer.

Frank said: 'D'you want me to clear out?'

Gloria hesitated. Then, quietly: 'I'll tell you when you come back. If you come back.'

'I don't think it's quite that dramatic. She says she just wants to talk to me about Dorothy and the years they spent together at Willow Square. I'm interested. Dorothy was my sister, nicht wahr? If it's all over between you and me, I might settle in Ida's part of the world.'

Frank laid the binoculars on the window sill and walked across the room to sit down next to Gloria on the sofa. They had become critical of each other, sometimes bickering, sometimes maintaining an introspective silence. Frank annoyed her with such barbs as 'You don't *know* anything, do you?' and she him with her heavy smoking, the smell of which was in her clothes and her hair. She never felt sorry for him, but increasingly he felt sorry for her.

He put his arm round her shoulders.

'You're a sad girl,' he murmured, his fond eyes on her sulky face and floury skin. 'There's always something missing, isn't there? A lot of people are like you. Life's never whole for them. I wish I could make you happy, Gloria.'

'You've tried,' Gloria replied, still reading the paper.

'I guess I lack the wherewithal.'

'I haven't heard it called that before. The luckiest people are the ones who have an abiding interest that they can pursue on their own – writing, pottery, dressmaking, anything. Mavis with her sketching is happier than I am.'

'Have you found someone to replace her, my love?'

'I've engaged an agency. Maybe they'll have better luck. When are you going to see this female?'

'Ida? I said I'd ring back after I'd spoken to you. Why not come?'

'I'm not invited.'

'Of course you are. I was only kidding.'

Frank kissed Gloria's cheek. Without looking at him, she turned a page.

'I'll drive you to Preston Station and pick you up when you come back. How long will you stay?'

'Depends how long the journey takes. Preston to London,

London to Andover, Andover to Wall Town, then a taxi. Two nights, maybe three. But I'm thinking about Mavis de Lapp and I think you are too, m'lady.'

'I can't expect her to go on coming here when the old couple need round-the-clock attention. She keeps dropping in, but I've told her she mustn't. I'll find someone.'

'I'll ring the station in a minute, then Green Eyes.'

'Your overnight bag.'

Gloria lowered the paper into her lap as Frank turned her head to kiss her pouty lips. He took gentle hold of her little hands, the hands with dimpled backs and bitten-down nails, and kissed her again with his eyes closed.

'I'll take my knuckledusters off and we'll go to bed for the afternoon,' she told him. 'By the time this Blanchard piece gets you between her thighs, you won't have enough wherewithal left to drown a flea.'

3

Frank had breakfast on the Preston–London train, luncheon at the Star & Garter in Andover, and dinner with Ida at Bytheway House. He wore his Chester Barrie suit with a starched white shirt and his Ancient Mariner's tie, but he kept his German grammar in his suitcase and was careful not to tell Ida that, in his opinion, the police should patrol on motor scooters instead of in cars, that proven killers and recidivists of all categories ought to be put to sleep, that the State should control human reproduction and that you can't change your nature but someone else can change it for you. This was a pity, because Ida enjoyed serious discussion and had grown to love knowledge for its own sake.

It is sometimes said that blue and green should never be seen, except upon a gypsy queen; but the Persian blue calf-length dress that Ida wore at dinner went just as well with her unforgettable green eyes as the peach cashmere two-piece she had worn when welcoming Frank towards the end of the afternoon.

She had personally conducted him to his room, which turned out to be a suite.

‘It was Robin’s flat,’ she explained, after Frank had stowed his suitcase and hung his Swallow mackintosh in the wardrobe. ‘Mine is next door. You met and talked with Robin, I think.’

‘At the Tiler’s Sword.’

‘The Tiler’s Toast. I have to tell you, Mr Hatfield, that Robin died ten days ago. Coronary thrombosis. I haven’t found his door key. Will that bother you tonight? No key?’

‘I shan’t even think about it, Mrs Blanchard.’

‘Will you call me Ida? I’m one of those rare people who like their own name.’

‘If you’ll call me Frank. Could I possibly have some coffee? I like it strong and sweet and without milk.’

‘Let’s go to my office and have it there, shall we?’

‘I’m very sorry to hear about Mr Blanchard.’

‘Robin.’

‘He was young to die like that. Had he a history of heart tremors?’

‘No. Never a murmur. That’s why it was such a terrible shock. Here we are. Please sit down. I’ll close the door.’

Ida went behind her desk and rang the kitchen to order coffee for two.

‘This time it *will* be Arabella who brings it. I didn’t introduce you to Robin when you and your wife were here because, to tell you the truth, I didn’t think the biography would amount to more than a pile of notes.’

‘Gloria isn’t my wife, Ida.’

‘Gloria’s her name? Another of my favourites. I used to think I’d like twin daughters and I’d christen them Gloria and Sylvia. Gold and silver. I’m old fashioned, Mr Hatfield.’

‘Frank. So am I, according to Gloria, and she disapproves. We had another of our rows just before I left to come here. She doesn’t like the way I dress. She called me a tailor’s dummy.’

‘And what’s wrong with that? I don’t like casual clothes on a man or a woman. Will you have a cigarette? No? Mind if I do? I’m like your sister, Frank, in as much as I love formality. Dorothy started me reading *The Times* before it became a Thomson newspaper in the mid-1960s and lost its unique character. She loved its seven stately columns, as she called them, the anonymity of its correspondents and contributors, and of course its impeccable taste and good manners. She liked the story of the *Times* editor in the 1930s who received a cable from his New York correspondent telling of the forthcoming marriage of Charlie Chaplin to Paulette Goddard. The editor replied "*The Times* is not interested in the marital affairs of Mr Chaplin". Help yourself to sugar.'

'Can you imagine today's editor saying that?' Frank asked, smiling. 'He'd be more likely to cable back "Dig up everything you can about the pair of them. Urgent!".'

'Scraps of information like that will help you with your biography. How much did Robin tell you when you met him at The Tiler's? I ask you that so as not to waste your time telling you things you already know. I believe he rang you several times afterwards too. You look mystified.'

'I think he's been pulling your leg, Mrs Blanchard.'

'Ida.'

'The biography isn't going ahead. When Gloria and I got back to Osprey Court the day after meeting Robin, we found a cable from the American publishers saying they'd hit a legal problem and the deal was off. Personally, I just think they'd got cold feet.'

'Oh, how awful for you! Did you tell Robin?'

'I rang him that night. I didn't want him rooting round for photographs of Dorothy and writing out his recollections of her, which is what he'd promised to do.'

'So does this mean the British edition is cancelled too?'

'British edition? A British edition was never proposed.'

Ida was beaming.

She leaned forward with: 'D'you like champagne, Frank?'

'Occasionally.'

'We're going to share a bottle of vintage tonight. Why? I'll tell you over dinner.'

Ida shared Gloria's love of flowers. They were in every room in her hotel, not least in the restaurant, where they graced every table and window sill. This was a room with smoke-blue seating and navy blue napery, its warmth coming from the redwood ceiling, walls of smooth buff brick and a mustard carpet and drapes. To soften the bareness of the walls, there were relief carvings in pear wood and a selection of framed samplers, which, to Ida's regret, were reproduction.

'Don't we curse ourselves when we remember some of the things we've thrown away?' Frank asked her, when they were smiling at each other across a table. 'After our mother died, Dorothy put a lot of things out with the rubbish. One of them was a sampler done by my grandmother in coloured silks on canvas. It read "Clara Minnie Richardson, her work, aged seven 1879. Consider the lilies of the field, how they grow: they toil not, neither do they spin".'

'And your sister threw that away? Most unlike her! Dorothy was very sensitive in matters of that sort; very appreciative of beauty.'

'I can see her now, holding it up for me to see and saying "You don't want this, do you?" Being only eighteen at the time, I said no.'

'Your sister opened my eyes to so many things, Frank - not just to the quirky old *Times* and the world of learning and sophistication that it reflected, but to the finer things of life in general. We often went to museums and concerts and the theatre together. I'd love to start reading again, but hoteliers get so little time to themselves, as you know, and I'd also like to learn to speak French properly. I remember a little of what Dorothy taught me and I trot it out when we have French guests.'

Ida detected a sympathetic listener in Frank Hatfield. Here was a calm and thoughtful man who, she felt, would assist and encourage her exploration of French. Robin had made fun of it. He had the English resentment, bordering on contempt, for adults bent on self-improvement. At best, they were freaks, at worst cads who were letting the side down.

Frank said: 'Our trade was seasonal at Redstone Bay. There was ample time for reading in the winter months. You make time for the things you really want to do. Although, having said that, I don't exercise nearly as much as I ought. Believe it or not, I was a keep-fit fanatic in my New Leaf days. I'm still a member of the health club at the Ninian Hotel, but I've hardly got beyond the swimming pool since I moved in with Gloria.'

'Is she a widow, Frank? She's very attractive, isn't she, in a dolly sort of way?'

'I'd say kittenish more than dolly. Her husband, Peter Raby, deserted her.'

'So did mine. His name was Billy Prince. In the eyes of the law, I suppose I'm still his wife, although I haven't seen him for twenty years and I hope I'll never see him again. I'm going to tell you now why we're celebrating with champagne.'

Frank waited. Moon-faced Ida was still smiling at him, her head tilted slightly backwards, heavy lids half-closing her eyes.

'It's because you're not going ahead with your biography of Dorothy. You wouldn't have been able to avoid mentioning Ida Prince and probably my whereabouts today and I was worried in case Billy read the book and decided to pay me a visit. He was a nasty little man, Frank, and he used to knock me about. These rings I'm wearing are the ones he gave me, because of course Robin and I weren't married. I was Mrs Blanchard because I like the name and because Billy wouldn't connect me with it. Also, it was good that the staff considered us man and wife. Cheers.'

'To the future!'

The couple touched glasses.

'I want to hear your history while we're together, Frank. Have you always lived with a woman or have you been married? D'you have any children? What are your plans for the future if, as I suspect, you and Gloria are going to separate?'

Frank was about to answer when Ida got ahead of him with: 'How long will you stay at Bytheway House? You're my guest, remember, and you're welcome to stay all week if you like.'

'I considered leaving tomorrow, Ida, after you've told me a little more about Dorothy.'

'Make it the day after and let me drive you to Andover to pick up the London train, so long as you don't mind being driven in a Riley Kestrel that has seen better days. Robin claimed he could get fifty miles an hour out of it given a strong tail wind. I'm afraid it hasn't been treated as a car ought to be treated.'

'I'd love to stay, Ida, and thank you for the offer of a lift.'

'There's to be a little celebration here tomorrow to mark the wedding anniversary of Hilary Blanchard, Robin's daughter by his first wife and therefore Dorothy's step-daughter.'

'Oh yes. Norah Blanchard mentioned she was on an extended holiday with her husband.'

'They flew home for Robin's funeral and they're still at Arrowcross Farm with Norah, trying to make up their minds whether to stay for good or go back to France and continue their safari. My hunch is they'll stay. Her husband will go over alone and bring back the furniture van they've been touring in. It's lovely having Hilary around again. We're like sisters. Always have been.'

'I hope she doesn't take exception to me because I'm Dorothy's brother.'

'I see Norah's been talking. Don't worry. Hilary's far too mature and well-educated to make you do penance for someone else's sins. She owns the riding school and livery stable that you must've seen at the side of this hotel. Her grandfather, Max Blanchard, had it built as a present for her.'

'A handsome present.'

'One that's been sorely neglected in Hilary's absence, between you and I. She left it in the care of a certain Nancy Carmine, but Nancy's too young and flighty for the part. You've only to count the love bites to see she should send the boyfriend home earlier. Norah's had more than a few dust-ups with Nancy over her slack management and bad time-keeping.'

'Is Norah coming to the do, Ida?'

'No, unfortunately. She isn't too well at the moment.'

4

Frank walked out of Preston Station expecting to find Gloria waiting in the Morgan. Instead, Mavis de Lapp flashed him from the BMW and pushed open the passenger door. They set off for Redstone Bay in darkness and heavy rain.

'Gloria went to Liverpool this morning to have her hair done,' Mavis explained. 'I looked in at the flat at four o'clock this afternoon, but no sign of her. I'm worried, Frank.'

'She'll be all right, Mavis. Gloria's not a simpleton.'

'I don't mean just now. When I called last night to collect her shopping list, I found her lying in front of the drawing room fire. She'd passed out.'

'I know she's back on the bottle, but she tells me to shut up when I try to talk her off it. I'm wasting my sweetness on the desert air.'

'You're too gentle, Frank, if you don't mind me saying so. She's still a child, remember.'

'I can't shake a rattle and pull faces at a woman of forty plus.'

'We were firm with her at Elderfield.'

'That's why she was there.'

'It was the only way to drain her.'

'Osprey Court isn't Elderfield, Mavis. What d'you want me to do? Smack her bottom and send her to bed? She'd be bouncing round like a rubber ball.'

'I don't know how Peter Raby handled her.'

'I don't think Peter Raby did. From what Gloria's told me, he was Scott Fitzgerald to her Zelda, except he wasn't interesting.'

'You won't desert her, will you, Frank? I shouldn't really speak to you like this, but I'm concerned for her safety.'

'I'll stay till she finds a replacement for you.'

'That could take weeks.'

Frank didn't answer.

Mavis said: 'We think Raby's out of prison. He was due for release on the thirteenth.'

'Unlucky for some.'

'Sorry?'

'It's what the caller says at bingo games. Housey-housey.'

'She's safe as long as you're there. But she's convinced you're going to leave her.'

'We've had our ups and downs lately, Mavis.'

'She's told me. What passes between the two of you is no business of mine. What becomes of Gloria is no business of mine either, except that after Mum and Dad she means more to me than anyone else in the world. It won't surprise you to hear, Frank, that she's given me this car. A BMW.'

Mavis was steering it now off the promenade and into the visitors' parking area facing the main entrance to Osprey Court. She stopped the engine and turned to Frank.

'I think Gloria's gone to the police,' she suddenly decided.

'What for? Protection against Raby? What can they do? He hasn't threatened her in any way, has he? She probably dropped in on a friend in Liverpool and stayed longer than planned. She'll be back now, Mavis, sitting watching television.'

'Gloria doesn't have friends. I'd feel easier if she did. She once said your sister was the only friend she ever had. It's ten past nine. If she's not at home, Frank, will you tell the police?'

'Certainly. If she's not in the flat, I'll be worried about her myself.'

'I've got this horrible feeling something's happened. I'll be round tomorrow, but I can't say when because of Mum and Dad.'

'Thanks for turning out, Mavis. Don't think about it. I'll look after her.'

The concierge was perched on his stool, his forearms extended on his counter, his grizzled head bent over the *Liverpool Echo* that lay between them. He didn't look up when Frank asked if Mrs Raby had returned.

'At seven twenty,' he grunted. Then, after a pause more eloquent than words: 'I put her car away for her.'

The long corridors were softly lit and thickly carpeted and silent save for the muffled sound of television behind three or four of the satinwood doors.

Gloria's was partly open.

Frank pushed it gently to its limit before stepping inside and putting his suitcase down. The only sound was that of gusting rain intermittently lashing the windows. All the interior doors stood open. With one exception, the rooms were deserted and in darkness. The exception was Gloria's bedroom.

'That you?' she murmured, without raising her head to see who was approaching.

She was curled up on her vast, silk-encased bed, with only a bedside lamp for illumination. Having kicked off her shoes and tossed her skirt over a chair, she was dressed only in black nylons with black suspenders, white knickers so tight they were like a second skin, and a black lace blouse.

'I'm mighty, mighty pissed,' she muttered, with her face in the pillow.

Frank stopped within three paces of her.

'I hope you didn't drive home like that, Gloria,' he said.

'Oh, it's you, is it?' Gloria groaned. 'Mr Health & Efficiency. Know what Raby would say? "Bravo! My little girl dodged the coppers. This calls for a drink". But not you. Not Frank Hatfield.'

'I'll make some coffee.'

'Oh, for God's sake! Make some coffee! What does a woman have to do to fire your boiler?' Gloria demanded. Turning onto her stomach, she thrust both hands under the pillow and started rubbing her nose in it. 'What did Green Eyes do? Stub her fag out on your bottom?'

'Your front door was open.'

'I'm expecting someone.'

'Raby?'

'You've won the silver rose bowl. What happened with Green Eyes? Did you get your leg over?'

'She came into my room when I was asleep and slipped in beside me.'

'By the look of that husband of hers, she's way out of practice. I'm not surprised Dorothy married him. I'll bet she kicked his arse a few times.'

'Robin's dead. I'm going to live with Ida.'

Gloria heaved herself onto one elbow and blew hair out of her eyes. It was the first time she'd looked at Frank.

'That – is – very – convenient,' she said, thoughtfully.

'How did you locate Raby?'

'I did the rounds of his old haunts, beginning at The Master Mason and ending at the house of one of the men who drove for him before he set fire to Raby Cars.'

'Bunny Littler?'

'You knew him. I'd forgotten.'

'He sometimes dropped in to read the paper when I had Peterkin's Gymnasium in Liverpool.'

'Bunny wasn't home, so I left a message with Agnes. He'll know where to find Raby.'

'You'll both want me out of the way.'

'Unless you fancy a three-in-a-bedder.'

'I'll stay at the Ninian.'

'Safer.'

Gloria lit a cigarette.

'You know my problem,' she murmured, with resignation in her voice. 'I need a high-voltage performer, not the standard male who gets back into his iron lung after a routine screw. Raby'll be shinning up lamp posts after his stretch behind bars.'

'Anything I can get you before I leave?'

Suddenly riled, Gloria shouted: 'Stop sounding like a manservant! You'd let me slap you.'

Frank turned to go, then paused.

'I'd just like to say thanks for the time we spent together,' he said. 'You helped me a lot, especially just after Cath took off with Dooley. I wish it'd been more fun for you.'

Quietly, solicitously, sounding now like an elder sister, Gloria asked if he would be all right.

'Will you?' he countered, with no less concern.

'I'll be as all right as I can hope to be in this world. I'll always be a stranger in it.'

'You know the Bytheway House number. It's on the pad. I'm going to buy the field behind the hotel and build a health club on it. Ida's quite tickled by the idea.'

'You're nice, Frank. Too nice. But not nice enough.'

'Have fun, Glorious. I know you will without my telling you.'

'Good luck, Frank. Aren't you going to call a taxi, dear?'

'Rain's stopped. I'd rather walk. I'll ring you tomorrow about collecting my kit.'

As he left the building, he passed behind an overdressed man standing facing the concierge, who had just picked up the internal telephone. Frank didn't need to be told his identity. Although there was space and to spare in the visitors' parking area, a chrome-drenched Pontiac had been left on double yellow lines.

It was a refreshing walk to the Ninian along the wet promenade, with the roaring sea to Frank's left, and to his right the lights of the guest houses reflected in the roofs of parked cars. A stiff, dry breeze made ropes slap against masts and flags flutter horizontally, like flies rubbing their front legs together. He felt more settled than at any time since the end of his years with Cathy. Once in his suite at the Ninian, he would order coffee and pork sandwiches, then telephone Ida to say he would be with her sooner than either of them expected.